"What are you doing here?"

"Getting a start on whatever it is you want me to do to you." The light in her car died off, leaving them alone in the night air. An owl hooted off in the distance over the sound of a diesel truck entering one of the back roads. With all the nighttime orchestra, Nate still heard her gulp, not in fear but uncertainty. Had she bitten off more than she could chew by bidding on him tonight?

"Are you going to tell me what you have in store for me now?" Nate asked. His eyes focused on her plump lips. She'd reapplied a layer of gloss during the ride over here because he knew he'd kissed off the strawberry flavor back at the club.

"In a rush to get back to Brittany?" Amelia countered. She pressed her manicured hand against his chest in a seeming attempt to put some space between them, but he felt the way her fingers lingered against his pecs.

Nate cocked his head to the side to study her face for a moment under the half-moon's light. "Babe, you've got me for a full week."

"And then?"

He grinned.

Dear Reader,

Welcome back to Southwood, Georgia. These are a few words Amelia Marlow never thought she'd hear.

R & R means something a little different in *His Southern Sweetheart*. For Amelia it stands for Reyes & Revenge. How can anyone want to seek revenge on such a hottie like Nate Reyes? Every time he did something sweet for Amelia, I just wanted to scream at her for being so mean.

Have I mentioned how I can take any situation and turn it into a love story? Combine this gift (as my friends and family validate this with a begrudging sigh) and my love for reality TV, and I thought I'd stir up a little romance for those who work behind the scenes.

His Southern Sweetheart came out of my love for reality TV and the unsung heroes—the television crew.

Carolyn Hector

R060b9 b3553

His
SOUTHERN
Sweetheart

Carolyn Hector

⬧ **HARLEQUIN**® KIMANI™ ROMANCE

Recycling programs
for this product may
not exist in your area.

ISBN-13: 978-0-373-86472-0

His Southern Sweetheart

Copyright © 2016 by Carolyn Hall

HARLEQUIN®
™ www.Harlequin.com

Printed in U.S.A.

Having your story read out loud as a teen by your brother in Julia Child's voice might scare some folks from ever sharing their work. But **Carolyn Hector** rose above her fear. She currently resides in Tallahassee, Florida, where there is never a dull moment. School functions, politics, football, Southern charm and sizzling heat help fuel her knack for putting a romantic spin on everything she comes across. Find out what she's up to on Twitter: @Carolyn32303.

Books by Carolyn Hector

Harlequin Kimani Romance

The Magic of Mistletoe
The Bachelor and the Beauty Queen
His Southern Sweetheart

Visit the Author Profile page at
Harlequin.com for more titles.

I would like to dedicate this book
to my one and only daughter, Haley, who binge-watches
all of my inspirational reality shows with me. Thanks,
Schmoopie!

Acknowledgments

Without the peace and quiet given to me by my son
and four nephews (coordinated by my husband),
I must acknowledge that without their cooperation,
I wouldn't get any writing done!

Chapter 1

With the four-hundred-thread-count eggshell-colored Egyptian cotton sheets tangled around her feet, Amelia Marlow kicked the material off the edge of the bed and wrapped her legs around the muscular calves of her partner. Their chests rose and fell in unison in the afterglow of their phenomenal evening of marathon lovemaking.

"So," they both breathed at the same time.

A sly grin spread across her face at the way the two of them had hit it off, from the time they met at the bar to the last wave of their orgasms. If she didn't know any better, she would have expected their first meeting to have been scripted. Six-foot-two with golden-bronze skin poured over steel muscles that no T-shirt could hide. His eyes were emerald green and had been focused on her the moment he filled the bar doorway. *Hot* didn't even begin to describe this man. Like every woman there, he'd caught her attention the minute he walked in. Who knew a couple of hours ago, when he'd walked directly over to her and offered to buy her a drink, that they'd end up with a nightcap in her hotel room? The first few moments, their conversation had been a string of flirty awkwardness and now here they were, speaking at the same time.

"You first," he said.

"Didn't I already?" Amelia replied with a purr.

He turned his head and pressed his lips against her bare shoulder. "I thought we might want to exchange names."

The point of a one-night stand meant no need to exchange names. She raised her brows. "You first."

"Nate," he said, squaring his jaw. "Nate Reyes."

The roll of his *R* across his tongue set a ripple of a reminder of his talents a few moments ago. "Amelia, Amelia Marlow."

Nate Reyes rolled to his right side, rested his head against his propped-up elbow and began to trace a pattern down from her chin to the center between her breasts with his forefinger. Subconsciously Amelia rested her hands against her stomach in attempt to make her breasts perky. The point of her elbow brushed against the hard contours of his ripped abs.

"And may I further say," she began, despite the heat rising up from her chest across her cheekbones, "this honestly isn't the type of thing I go around doing."

His response came in a casual shrug. "Whatever the reason, I'm glad you did. I enjoyed myself this evening."

"Me, too."

The last time Amelia took a break from her job was probably never. Ever since the world had become enamored with reality shows, being on top of her game had become a necessity. As a field producer for MET, she'd found that personal relationships dwindled. Right now she was on the fast track for a seat on the throne as one of Multi-Ethnic Television's future showrunners. Amelia busted her ass as a runner, becoming a field producer, following around the station's biggest reality celebrities as they tweeted across the globe. Some days her current job seemed more like a glorified babysitter. Reality TV celebrity Natalia Ruiz was becoming bored with being followed 24/7 for her hit show, *Azúcar.* When a star was bored, so were the viewers. Amelia shook her head to get her job out of her mind. Why think about work when a smoking-hot man lay naked beside her?

"I want to see you again."

"I am only in Atlanta for the weekend. I'm checking out tomorrow." Amelia shook her head left to right. Strands of hair brushed against her dewy skin. The cute flip hairstyle she'd gotten done today now flopped. *He was worth it.*

"So am I." Nate rolled onto his back. "We need to do this again, soon."

Amelia shifted to her side and faced him. She wished she hadn't kicked the sheets to the floor. Instead of hiding her not-so-toned frame with covers, she curled her knees up to her chest as much as her non-yoga-perfected body would allow. *Why hadn't she taken some lessons during the* Azúcar *episode with Natalia?*

"My schedule is demanding," Amelia began. She had no time for relationships with her jet-setting schedule. The red light of the digital clock on the nightstand on the other side of the bed read sometime after midnight. She was surprised she hadn't heard from her executive producer or the cameramen. Did she seriously get a few hours to herself? Well, she countered herself, not all by herself.

Nate lifted his almond-shaped eyes to hers. The faint smell of coconut rum lingered on his full lips. He had a low Caesar-style haircut and the most delectable caramel skin. A half sleeve of petroglyphs or a tribal tattoo decorated the length of his muscular bicep. Thanks to interning as a part of the camera crew for MET's show featuring tattoo artists, she understood the sun design to be part of a Taíno Indian culture. Amelia's heart fluttered with excitement for remembering the detail.

"So this is seriously going to be a one-night stand?"

"I believe we need to think of tonight as one special moment." Amelia sighed. "I need to get back to work."

"It's after midnight." Nate propped himself up on his elbow and raised his brows.

"Sorry," she mumbled, contorting the upper half of her body over the side of the bed. Her hands searched around on the floor for the slacks she'd kicked out of and came across her navy, polka-dot bra and panties. As she tucked the undergarments in, her fingertips brushed across the soft beige carpet, reading it like braille for the pants until she found the hem strewn halfway across her hotel floor. The material of her pants was rolled over a shoe or a heel. She was glad the lamp lights were off. She'd have hated to see clearly what the room looked like. As it was, the full moon's light spilled from the balcony's open drapes and offered a view of the wreckage they'd created from tearing off each other's clothes. She was sure they'd knocked everything off the dresser in their state of passion.

"What kind of work forces you out after midnight?" asked Nate before choking on a stifled laugh. "Wait, do I want to know?"

From her awkward angle, Amelia playfully tapped her foot against his broad chest. He captured her by the heel and kissed her big toe. Amelia jumped forward, found her cell phone and sat upright in the bed. She swore as the blue light indicating a message flashed furiously. The mattress behind her dipped and the heat from Nate's body warmed her backside when he pulled her into his arms. As she tried to read her messages on her phone, his arms caressed the swell of her breasts. Amelia sunk into the warmth of him. Perhaps she had a few more minutes to respond to the swelling erection pressed against her backside. A rueful smile crept across her face, knowing she probably needed to stock up on sex. Lord only knew when she'd meet a man like this again.

The trail of kisses he left on her collarbone sizzled against her skin. Desire throbbed through every inch of her body. The shrill of her phone filled the silent room, shocking her system much like a bucket of ice dumped on her.

"Do you need to answer your phone?" he asked, kissing the tip of her earlobe and moving toward the side of her mouth. His large hands moved down her rib cage to the V of her thighs.

"No," she gasped. The phone stopped ringing. A half second later someone banged on her hotel door. Amelia turned the lights on by the switch beside her bed. "But I must answer that."

"Should I hide?" he asked, making no move to do so or effort to cover his naked and ready body.

The pounding on the door rattled the frame, the extra lock jingling against the bolt. Amelia jumped into her slacks, sans undergarments, turning her back to him as she zipped and buttoned herself. She cast a glance over her shoulder and raised a brow. "Are you in the habit of finding women who make you hide afterward?"

"Touché."

Her phone began to ring again and this time when she glanced Natalia's face appeared on the caller ID. From the other side of the door, her current boss banged and began to yell her name. Amelia's eyes cringed with embarrassment as William Vickers cursed.

"Oh, hell no." Nate moved from the bed. Naked, he stormed toward the door with his hand stretched outward for the doorknob. "Boyfriend or not, no man should speak to you this way."

"Wait!" Partly panicked and partly impressed with Nate's chivalry, Amelia rolled her eyes and sighed. She missed the gallantry of men these days. In the production world, manners were seriously lacking. "He's kind of my boss, not my boyfriend, and if you don't mind, I need you to step into the bathroom."

"Why?"

Amelia's eyes drifted to his naked, hard frame. It'd be a shame to have to cover or hide a beautiful body such as his. "Whatever's going on with my job, I don't want him thinking it was because of a romp in the hay."

For half a minute, while William continued to knock, Nate stood in front of her, staring her down. Reluctantly he turned to head toward the bathroom. The view from behind was just as beautiful. "And it's a bed, not hay," he mumbled before closing the door.

Once the other door clicked closed, Amelia crossed the room and opened the door just a crack. "Are you crazy?"

William, mobile showrunner of MET, stood stock-still, hand raised in the air. Still dressed in a pin-striped business suit from the editing dinner, he narrowed his dark eyes at Amelia. He craned his neck to try and peer in through the crack she kept open. "What the hell are you up to?" His bulbous nostrils flared with his question.

"Sleeping?"

"You're a field producer of a reality show where it is your *job* to follow your star around."

"And she's asleep," Amelia gritted out between her teeth.

Of all the people to come and tell her how to do her job, William standing here irritated her the most. They'd both started out at MET as runners for cable television reality shows, doing errands for the directors, showrunners and field producers. They'd both vied for the same executive producer opening. And while William might have been the *mobile* showrunner with all the power to make creative and directive decisions, everyone on set listened to Amelia. She and her group of cameramen had their jobs down pat. William wanted this assignment for the chance to work with the Caribbean royal family, the Ruizes. Everyone at MET wanted the chance to head over to the Ruiz compound in San Juan, Puerto Rico, to film footage for *Azúcar*. Thanks to the quick friendship she and Natalia had forged, Amelia had earned the honors to work with the icon for the commercial.

"You sure?" William bared his teeth while his upper lip curled. His puffy hand thrust forward, shoving his cell phone toward her face. Amelia's already blown-out back ached from the base of her spine as she leaned backward to focus on the picture of Natalia having an intimate dinner with a bearded stranger. The corners of William's mouth turned upward and his eyes roamed the part of her body visible through the door. Amelia reached for the phone but William pulled it away. "You dropped the ball in order to get your *beauty* rest."

"She said she was going to bed and I am allowed some personal time."

"For as long as you've been babysitting her," William gritted, "when did she say she wanted a quiet evening?"

Jesus, no wonder Natalia had been so sweet this eve-

ning. How long had she been planning this rendezvous? And who was this mystery man? Amelia documented Natalia's life practically twenty-four hours out of the day. She'd never seen the man on the screen. Only the side of his face showed from William's phone, but Amelia knew if she waited long enough, more pictures would be plastered over the internet. "Where is she now?"

"Hell if I know. Whoever is blogging said the two of them parted and went their separate ways after dinner. Damn shame we didn't get any of this on film. Do you understand what our ratings would be like? If Natalia's ready to start dating, we could have a bachelorette spin-off."

Ratings were not an issue for Amelia as long as Natalia stayed interested in being in the public eye. Lately, however, she hadn't enjoyed it too much—neither of them. The closer she grew to Natalia, the more Amelia liked her. They were friends. Unlike Natalia, Amelia was a far cry from an heiress.

"Are you even listening to me?" William's bark snapped Amelia out of her pity party.

She straightened her spine and shook her head while closing her door. "Give me a minute and I'll go find her." The door clicked closed, locking William out of her life for a brief moment.

"She's not in her room," William shouted from the other side of the door.

Dressed, Nate stepped out from the bathroom. Amelia's heart sunk with disappointment. She gave him a half smile and inhaled deeply as he crossed the room toward her.

"I take it you've got to go?"

"Sorry," she mumbled, her eyes focused on the center of his defined chest. The maroon V-neck T-shirt he wore hugged his pecs and arms. The first thing about him she'd spotted was his bicep when he reached across the bar downstairs to pay for a round of drinks. She'd always adored a man with nice arms.

"Did you at least enjoy yourself?" Nate asked, stopping inches from her. His gaze focused on her lips.

"Hell yeah." Amelia anticipated his hug and opened her arms. Somehow being in his embrace she felt safe, warm, as if everything was going to be okay—but it wasn't. Her tryst this evening might come with a cost—her job. *Was he worth it?* Nate's arms closed tighter around her waist and he effortlessly lifted her into the air while planting a stream of kisses along her collarbone. Goose bumps began to swarm her forearms. A wicked wave of passion fluttered between her legs. *Dear Lord Jesus, yes, this man was worth it.*

"I plan on seeing you again," Nate declared, setting her on her feet.

"I wouldn't bet the farm." Amelia half smiled. "I am a pretty busy woman."

"I like farms." Nate perked up. His emerald green eyes lit up with curiosity. "What do you know about farms?"

"Boy, please," she said, pushing at his chest playfully. "We may have just met, but don't be fooled by the manicure. Trust me, I spent my summers on my grandmamma's farm in rural Georgia eating peaches straight from the tree."

"How rural?" Her body moved forward when Nate tugged at the button of her slacks. "I love me a country girl."

"We're talking one streetlight downtown, you blink and you miss it."

"Keep talking." He stroked his long index finger against her earlobe and down the curve of her jaw. "You're turning me on."

"I wish I had the time."

"We have to do this again," he said, leaving a trail of kisses where his fingers had touched moments ago.

Flames of desire flickered in the pit of her stomach. A television pitch popped into her head:

Dear MET executives,
Instead of airing a highlight segment on the best
fights of our reality shows, how about the best hook-
ups of seasons past? Better yet, best one-night stands,
complete with a where-is-he-now segment.
Sincerely,
Amelia

The phone in her hand began to ring. This time, instead of Natalia's face, Amelia's mother's face appeared. Amelia's heart thumped against her rib cage. Cynthia Marlow never called after nine. "Maybe. I'll leave my info at the desk, but right now I've got to take *this* call."

"Heavy is the head that wears the crown," he teased, leaning forward to brush a kiss against her cheek. Any other given time, Amelia would have extracted her business card, her real one, and encouraged him to definitely use the number. But right now, for her mama to call after midnight, something was up.

"I'll let you take your call," he said as he reached behind her to open the door, "and get some coffee for us."

Amelia half smiled while watching him walk away, appreciating the view. She closed the door behind her and exhaled a deep breath. What on earth had she been thinking tonight?

"Amelia? Amelia, darling, are you there?"

For a moment Amelia had forgotten her mother until she heard her father, Howard Marlow, question whether or not she was on the line. She tapped the speaker button and fanned her face with her free hand. "Hi, Mama, it's late, what's going on?"

"Amelia, honey, it's your grandmamma."

Nate Reyes stood by his motto, *No complications.* Yet, since his encounter with the reality show producer a week ago, his life seemed anything but. He wasn't supposed to daydream about what she was doing. He wasn't supposed to stop being interested in other women. Yet she consumed him.

"Can we stop this now, Uncle Nate?"

The words registered in Nate's brain, but he did not acknowledge them until his niece Kimber exhaled a droll sigh. As he tried not to laugh at Kimber's irritation, the pink feathers of the boa he wore around his neck flittered and stuck to the pink lip gloss he'd worn at the insistence of his other niece, five-year-old Philly. Nate glanced up from the tiny pink porcelain cup of air-tea in time for the dramatic eye roll. For the last forty minutes, Kimber had refused to partake in the semiformal tea party her sister had set up for them.

"Sorry, *Tío* Nate," Kimber corrected herself with a heavy Spanish accent and clearer sarcasm.

In the span of eight months, Nate had uprooted his life to move from Atlanta to settle down in Southwood, Georgia, to raise his two nieces in their childhood home after his brother Ken and sister-in-law, Betty, had passed away. Named legal guardians, Nate and his older brother, Stephen, didn't have a fight on their hands for custody of their nieces. Betty's parents were too old to take care of the girls and Nate's parents lived on Villa San Juan, a small island off the northwest coast of Florida.

Between him and Stephen, they'd seamlessly transitioned themselves into a daily part of the girls' lives by bringing their real estate and contracting business down South. With the help of Stephen's soon-to-be fiancée, Lexi Pendergrass, the clan now had a stable touch of femininity. They'd even managed to take Kimber and Philly on an overdue visit to their paternal grandmother when Nate's mother had noticed the lack of Puerto Rican cultural influence in the way the girls were growing up. And somehow the blame was placed on Nate and Stephen.

"My bad," Nate said, setting the dainty cup on its matching saucer with a clatter. He shifted in the small pink seat. Truth be told, he wanted to end this activity but he'd promised Philly a tea party if she could spend one full day without wearing her well-earned tiara from her beauty pageant last weekend. People in Southwood thought Philly waltzing around town with her pageant crown was cute, but if she scratched the back windows of his SUV any more he was going to have to replace them. Thanks to the heaviness of the twelve-inch Swarovski tiara, the walls in the house leading up the stairs were scraped. Everyone in the family had scratches on their arms from Philly standing too close and turning her head. Even the wooden headboard of Philly's twin bed suffered from deep grooves because she slept with the crown.

"May I be excused now?" asked Kimber.

"Are you finished with your tea?" Nate asked with a lopsided grin. He leaned forward to peer into his oldest niece's cup, which she angled toward him with another eye roll.

"You didn't finish your cookies." Philly pointed out the stack of burnt premade desserts the woman in the grocery store had promised would be easy to make.

Nate cleared his throat and nodded his head toward the cookies. Kimber's mouth widened with disbelief.

"This is beyond punishment," Kimber mumbled. "This is cruel and unusual."

Burning the cookies had totally been his fault. His mind had been elsewhere—in Atlanta and on the sexy producer who'd fled the minute she had the chance. Of course, finding her wouldn't be hard. He knew Natalia Ruiz personally and if he didn't his media connections at MET would have come in handy.

Nate's mind breezed over Amelia once again. Tomorrow would make a week since being with her and she still hadn't gotten out of his system. The original plan in Atlanta had been to distract her at the bar, buy her a drink or something in order for Stephen to speak with a potential client. Taking her to bed the same night—well, those were the perks of being a great wingman.

A set of keys jingled at the front door and automatically Philly's face lit up with excitement. A deep "aha" came from Stephen Reyes at the bar separating the dining room and kitchen. He entered; the front door slammed shut and moments later in walked the future Mrs. Stephen Reyes, Lexi Pendergrass, who shook her head in preparation at the banter.

"I expected you to teach them how to gamble," said Stephen, standing at the bar and staring into the breakfast nook in a two-piece gray suit with a gray-and-blue paisley tie loosened at the throat, "but a tea party?"

"C'mon, bruh, you know when a five-year-old asks you to play tea party, you damn well better play tea party."

"Oooh," Kimber and Philly chorused.

"Go ahead and put your cash in the swear jar," ordered Lexi.

For a split second Nate scowled in Lexi's direction as she pulled Philly's chair away from the table. Thanks to the rule Lexi had installed in her pageant dress shop, the swear jar had now made its way to the marble kitchen counter. Nate stood and stepped over his mini chair. Stephen followed him into the kitchen as if to make sure Nate extracted a dollar for the jar. So far they had enough money to take a trip down to Puerto Rico.

"I expected more from you," Stephen pretended to scold.

"Really?" Nate raised a brow. "You expected more even after asking me for a favor last week?" Albeit, Stephen never asked Nate to go such the distance.

Screwing the top back on the jar he replaced it back on the counter before reaching into the fridge for a cold beer. Lexi appeared in the doorway with Philly on her hip and let out a low whistle. "Do I even want to know?"

"No," Stephen and Nate chorused.

"Sounds like my cue to leave." Kimber pushed away from the small table. "Uncle Stephen?"

Stephen made an elaborate show of ignoring his niece and keeping his focus straight ahead on Nate, who bit the inside of his cheek to keep from laughing. Kimber had Stephen wrapped around her finger.

Sucking her teeth, Kimber remembered. "*Tío* Stephen?"

"Yes, darling?"

Nate refused to be putty in Kimber's hand and wasn't remotely fooled by the sugary tone in her voice. He gave her the props for having the nerve to sweet-talk Stephen after all the scheming she'd done this summer. Recently, Kimber thought she could get away with the bait-and-switch boyfriend trick, saying she was dating an overly studious classmate instead of a football player jock, for fear they wouldn't approve. They didn't at first, but Nate and Stephen were growing fond of Philip. On top of the boyfriend issue, Kimber stole a racy dress from Lexi's Grits and Glam Gowns boutique in order to impress the jock. He already knew what Kimber was going to ask. Stephen may have laid down the law, but Nate made sure she followed it.

"Am I still grounded?"

"Yes."

Kimber grunted and balled up her fists as she spun around to stomp up the kitchen steps. The glass patio door leading out to the pool shook. Only when Kimber's door slammed shut did Nate and Stephen start to laugh.

"That's your niece," said Stephen as he shook his head.

"Oh, sure." Nate sighed. "When they're good, they're your nieces, but when they're bad, they're mine. This is the thanks I get for staying home with them all day long cooking and cleaning?"

Stephen turned and faced Lexi. "Here we go."

"Look, I am the one getting the kids ready for school, making sure they have their breakfast—"

"Is your cooking really a selling point?" asked Stephen.

Nate restrained the urge to flip his brother the middle finger. "Let's not forget all the back-to-school forms I've been filling out all day long. I swear I provided this same information back in January. We have two kids in the school system. Why can't there be one form online for them? My damn hand hurts."

"Well." Lexi chuckled. "Good luck trying to reform Southwood. In the meantime, I'm going to put our beauty queen to bed. Tomorrow, Nate, you and I can get a mani-pedi. Sound good?"

"Funny," Nate said, realizing being a third wheel was becoming a nuisance.

"You may want to take her up on her offer, Nate," said Stephen. "Do something together tomorrow."

"Tomorrow is Thursday. I've got to take the girls school shopping so I'm not fighting the crowds who also waited until the last minute."

"I can do it," offered Lexi. She gave Stephen a wink and Nate rolled his eyes. The main reason the two of them had first met was because Stephen had jumped the gun over the racy dress Kimber wore. He assumed when Kimber said she got the dress from Lexi's boutique that Lexi had sold it to her. "You guys discuss it. The queen and I are going upstairs."

As Lexi passed by Stephen, he reached out and swatted her behind. "Later, I get to put my beauty queen to bed."

Nate pretended to gag. Stephen did not show as much constraint with flipping him off. "Domestic life looks good on you, bruh," Nate teased, passing through the kitchen to the open French doors to the dining room. He sat down at the large maple table.

"Thanks. You ought to try it someday."

The image of a pair of copper-hued legs wrapping around his waist entered his mind. "One day."

"So for now you're still on the market?"

Nate did not like the tone in his brother's voice. They might not be twins, but Nate understood how Stephen's mind worked. First he'd try to talk about how something was a great idea and the next thing Nate knew, he'd be volunteering to do his bidding. Nate already knew the stakes.

Earlier today at the grocery store, a few of the ladies he lunched with after church had asked if he planned on doing the fall bachelor auction Saturday night. Proceeds from the benefit went toward supplies for the local schools in four counties, affectionately referred to as Four Points. This fall marked the first time his nieces started school without their parents. The kids had adjusted to their new life and Nate liked to take the credit for their stability.

He also saw himself as the charitable type in most cases, but something about being on stage and having women bid on him frightened him. Since being here the last few months, he'd been the shiny new toy all the single ladies—and not all single—wanted to play with. The last thing he wanted was for any of these Southern belles to have to expose themselves by making a spectacle while bidding on him. Lord knew these ladies were not quite proper behind closed doors.

"Slow your roll," Nate half grinned. "I know where you're going with this."

"Then you'll understand the money you'll bring in will go toward the school."

"And time," Nate added. "This auction offers up services of forty hours of my time. God only knows what will be expected of me if certain people bid on me."

"So you'll fix things here and there," said Stephen. "Business is slow and it's only forty hours. I am sure I can handle things."

Nate didn't have much to do besides refurnishing Lexi's shop, which she was in no rush to open. He took a seat. "I've been in town a lot longer than you. All of a sudden you care?"

"If I plan on staying here and raising my family," Stephen said with a sly smile.

"Are you trying to tell me Lexi's pregnant?" Nate asked, leaning forward and widening his eyes. He lowered his voice in case Lexi could hear from upstairs in Philly's room. "You sly old dog."

"No." Stephen frowned, then shook his bald head back and forth. "I am talking about the future. Our future."

Prior to Ken and Betty passing away, Nate had worked alongside his brothers in a lucrative real estate and contracting business based in California. They provided the perfect homes and locations for Hollywood directors to film movie scenes. When Ken met his wife and started their family, he moved to Betty's hometown in Southwood, Georgia. Nate and Stephen, wanting to be near their brother, then moved Reyes Realty and Contracting closer without actually being in Southwood. Atlanta, a rising home for television and film, was a perfect location. When Ken passed away, they realized that, in order to better care for their nieces, they had to commit to moving to Southwood.

"Whatever you're planning, stop."

"Don't you want to be a part of the community?" asked Stephen.

"I am, more so than you." Nate shuffled cards one good time, then stacked them in the center of the table. The back of the chair supported his weight when he leaned backward to reach in his pocket for his cell phone. Four missed texts in the last hour from three different women, one a bit antsier than the others. Brittany Foley, his after-school special. Nate grinned. The pre-K teacher had worked with Philly during the transition after Ken died. She also worked on Nate in a more intimate way. He scratched his chin and the hairs where the beard he hadn't bothered to shave away all week tickled his fingers.

Stephen sighed. "Hooking up with all the ladies in town is not considered being part of the community."

"Whatever," he mused. None of the women seemed to compare to Amelia. He dodged them at after-school pickup, went different directions down the aisle in the grocery store and hadn't paid attention to any of his text messages. Prior to Amelia, his messages never went unread. Now, eh. What was wrong with him?

"Speaking of your service…" Stephen cleared his throat before folding his arms across his chest. "You've been staying in all week. Something you need to tell me?"

"Like what?" Leave it to Stephen to pay attention to this part of his personal life. When they were kids, Nate had been the nosy one.

"Like something about the woman you distracted for Natalia."

"Yeah, so much for the private conversation. You two were blasted all over the internet." The corners of Nate's mouth turned upside down. The checkout lines were filled with photographs of Stephen and their childhood-friend-turned-reality-star. The guys knew Natalia way before she and her family became household names.

Stephen waved off the Nate's guilt. "Lexi's fine and we've never been better. I have you to thank. Natalia's looking to leave show business and we're in charge of finding a remote place for her."

"You're welcome, I guess."

"Want to talk about the woman on your mind?"

"Hell no," Nate snapped and pushed away from the table.

Stephen threw his hands in the air in surrender. "Sorry, don't bite my head off."

Nate waved his cell phone in the air and offered a cocky grin. "I am going to get back into the swing of things."

"Attaboy." Stephen began to give a slow clap. "I'm proud of you."

Lexi bounced down the stairs. Her eyes looked between the two brothers. "Great. You agreed to do it."

"Do what?" asked Nate. His eyes cut between his brother and Lexi.

Stephen pushed away from the wall and cleared his throat. "We hadn't gotten around to that part yet."

"What haven't we gotten around to, big brother?" Nate leaned into the back of the chair, resting his long legs on the seat of the chair across from him.

Lexi stepped forward and flashed her tiara-winning smile. "We signed you up for the bachelor auction Saturday."

Chapter 2

Grandmamma was ornery as ever, complaining every time the nurses brought a meal. The broken leg she'd sustained while trying to climb the stairs at her house did not improve her sour disposition. Either the food lacked seasoning or it had been cooked too long. After receiving the news of her grandmother's fall down the steps, Amelia requested a few days off from work. Amelia had spent her first two days in Southwood at the Four Points General Hospital, listening to her complain about her leg not needing to be in traction and inquiring about the ages of the doctors coming into her hospital room. If she wasn't at the hospital Amelia had been moving things around at Grandmamma's home, where she'd stayed. She'd seen no need in looking up old friends: she had none. Her cousin Cay would be back from her family vacation this weekend and would be able to help with the house. Grandmamma needed to accept the fact that she was getting old and the

steps were too much for her. As much as she'd dreaded
being called in to the head office in Orlando, Florida, she'd
almost welcomed the chance to get away from the hospital.

Seated on the black leather couch in front of the receptionist's desk at MET Studios, Amelia crossed one leg over
the other. The drive from Southwood to Orlando took four
hours, but the day trip barely wrinkled her clothes. The
black pencil skirt she wore today stretched against the back
of her thighs as her foot began to twitch back and forth.
She wore her brown hair in a French twist; she'd limited
the amount of mascara she wore in case she cried today,
and wore a light yellow, opal-colored blouse guaranteed
to not allow her to sweat in this oppressive, never-ending,
Southern summer heat. Thanks to a layer of anti-bite nail
polish, she at least did not gnaw on her fingernails. Unlike
the other sixteen floors below, which moved at the speed
of light with reporters, producers, editing rooms, writers
all trying to get their say and test kitchens, the top floor
of Kelly Towers remained quiet. A light laughter filtered
from the office next door to the boss. Amelia focused on
the executive assistant, Rory Montgomery, who was seated
at her desk and circling her index finger in the air to wind
up her phone call with whomever was on the other line.

When she finished with her call, Rory opened the glass
door to her own office and inclined her head for Amelia
to enter.

"Jesus, Amelia, I've never seen you so nervous," Rory
commented.

In their ten years of knowing each other since freshman year at Florida A&M University, Rory might not have
seen Amelia in too many nervous situations. As a budding
young journalism major, Amelia had never found the time
to think about her nerves. *There's always a first for everything.* Amelia offered a half smile to the young recep-

tionist at the desk as she passed by her circular desk and prayed her bundles of nerves weren't so obvious.

Amelia had been on this floor when she came in for a job interview. After learning Amelia had earned her master's in journalism from the University of Alabama, Rory had insisted on her friend applying for one of the producing jobs. Tired of being a glorified coffee girl for various production crews, Amelia took Rory up on the suggestion. Since being hired, Amelia had avoided the boss's floor like a juvenile avoided the principal's office. The friends never met in Rory's office and now today they were going to have a casual meeting in here: Rory, Amelia and Christopher Kelly—the head man in charge.

"Relax." Rory closed the door behind them and waved toward the two empty seats in front of her large black cherrywood desk. "You act like you're about to walk the plank."

The familiar diploma hung over the crimson wall above Rory's computer. A black cherrywood bookshelf held several books, but Amelia mainly focused on the old photographs of Rory's accolades from her time at MET. There was even a photograph of the two of them, arm in arm the first day of their freshman year, right next to one of the two of them at graduation. Looking at the pictures now, Amelia saw a resemblance between them. They had the same bobbed hairstyle popular at the time, and they both shared the same dark brown locks. Everyone always asked if they were related. Both women were athletically built, though neither of them played a sport, and had the same pecan skin color. Amelia liked to party, whereas Rory stayed in the dorm room to study.

"I'm not?" Amelia shook her head.

"You're my girl." Rory winked. "I'm not going to let you get thrown under the bus." Because of her genuineness, professionalism and commonsensical approach to work, Rory enjoyed her—technically, *their*—boss's trust and wielded a certain influence over him.

"William's already called?" Amelia asked. Of course the mobile showrunner ratted her out in order to kiss up to MET execs.

"He called the minute he left your hotel room." Rory rolled her eyes with disdain for William. "I warned Christopher about leaving his phone on at night."

"Oh?" Amelia's brows rose and a side grin began to form. "William didn't interrupt anything between you two, did he?"

"Don't start." Rory laughed. "We are strictly platonic."

As a person who observed people for a living, Amelia had picked up on some of the kind things Christopher Kelly did for Rory, but she decided to keep her thoughts to herself. She'd never heard of many bosses who randomly surprised their assistants with their favorite flowers or took them to family retreats. Of the few boyfriends Amelia had had in life, she'd only met the parents of one of them once and that wasn't by choice—they'd lived across the street from her family for a while.

"Okay." Amelia decided to drop it. Thinking of Rory's perfect life only shined a light on Amelia's glaringly imperfect one.

"Care to tell me who the guy was?" Rory asked.

"A lady doesn't kiss and tell."

Rory peered around Amelia's frame. "I don't see one, so dish."

"His name is Nate." Amelia relaxed in her seat, spreading her fingers around the cushion of the blush chair.

"Okay," Rory said slowly. "Nate what? And what does he do?"

"Reyes." Amelia rolled her *R* the way he did.

A squeal escaped Rory's mouth. "You naughty girl!"

"Whatever. I was due a night."

"I couldn't agree with you more." Rory nodded. "He must have been something special, huh?"

For some reason Amelia didn't want to reveal too much, not even to her margarita gal pal. "I don't know, and I'm not even sure if I am going to ever see him again. I got the call about my grandmamma and pretty much hightailed it out of the room."

"I'm sorry, sweetie."

Amelia shrugged her shoulders. "It is what it is, and I am not cut out for relationships."

"Because you love your job so much?"

A coy smile spread across Amelia's face; she resisted emitting a maniacal laugh accompanied with a sinister rubbing of hands together. "I was going to say because I get to manipulate people's lives, but let's go with your answer."

A cool breeze touched the back of Amelia's neck and the sound of the phones ringing amplified behind her. The door opened and before she had the chance to turn around, Christopher Kelly stood beside her, hand stretched out. Amelia rose, not sure if she needed to curtsy or bow. The Kelly family was famous around the state. Cal Kelly, Christopher's father, was an unchallenged state senator. His brother Mason was climbing the political ladder; another brother, Drew, was a doctor in the military and a hero for saving lives, and then there was Jared, the playboy war vet who worked for the DEA. Christopher's mother, Maggie Kelly, was the only daughter of a pioneering movie producer who'd made the multicultural films Hollywood wouldn't. Amelia had always admired Maggie Kelly for taking over her father's business and building it into a multimillion-dollar corporation. To say Amelia was star-struck was an understatement.

"Mr. Kelly," Amelia said as she decided to stand, misjudged his tall height and ended up hitting him in the lower abdomen with the top of her head as she stood up. "I'm so sorry," she squealed with a flinch. Tears of embarrassment threatened to test her waterproof mascara.

"Amelia." Rory sighed. "Relax. Chris, you remember meeting Amelia Marlow. Amelia, this is obviously Christopher Kelly."

"Yes, I recall our interview," Christopher said with a charming smile. He kept one hand in the left pocket of his light gray slacks while he shook her hand with the right. A crisp white Oxford was unbuttoned at this throat. "You're one of our promising producers."

"Thank you for noticing. And I've admired all of your work, too."

"Well, let's save some of that admiration until after this meeting."

After her visit with her boss, Amelia went back to her studio apartment to pack a few things. Who ever heard of mandatory sick leave? Instead of being suspended, the boss strongly insisted Amelia take the time off to care for her grandmother in Southwood, away from Orlando and the studio. In a way, she should have been relieved for not having a suspension on her spotless work record.

Mr. Kelly chalked up the missed opportunity for this golden moment of reality TV due to her being overworked. He told her to take this opportunity to spend quality time with her grandmother and not concern herself with work—at least not for a few weeks or until she got her grandmother situated. He meant well, but work was her life. To top things off, the landlord caught her coming down the steps and stopped her to let her know about the impending increase in rent. So in four months she needed to decide if she wanted to renew her soon-to-be expensive apartment, where she rarely spent more than four days in a row, or take part of her time off to try and find a new place to move. Right now, she had enough to do.

Apparently, her starlet, Natalia, had refused to come out of the bathroom to be filmed. This latest incident in *Azúcar* only validated Amelia's standing in the company. The commercial shoot for their number one show was on hold without Amelia being there to lay down the law. Natalia had refused to be filmed and spent her days in the bathroom, where the cameramen would not follow. They'd originally come to Atlanta to shoot a commercial, and the management team for the ad agency hired to create the latest business adventure, Azúcar Perfume, was gravely behind schedule. Amelia had granted one last favor to MET by making the trip back to Atlanta to explain to her star why she wouldn't be able to work with her for a while.

"You're so sweet for coming to see me face-to-face." Natalia unclipped her thumbtack-sized microphone off the collar of her yellow blouse.

Amelia's eyes glanced toward the mini-microphone and cringed. Her life's work had been catching every moment for reality TV. How in the hell was she going to last in Southwood for the duration of her grandmother's rehabilitation? "Of course I came to see you face-to-face. We're friends and I firmly believe an explanation is best that way."

"Well, I for one I can't begin to tell you how sorry I am," Natalia wailed as she fell against the oversize makeup chair in her Atlanta hotel suite. The stylist applying the black eyeliner messed up and left a streak of makeup along Natalia's temple. According to William's snide remarks, today was the first day Natalia had decided to put on makeup, thanks to the heads-up of Amelia's arrival. Since Natalia had gone on her impromptu strike, there had been no grand openings or appearances to promote Azúcar Perfume, the latest business project for the Ruiz family, so filming was at a standstill.

Even with no formal announcement, Amelia still knew the show was about to go on. Most people, like Amelia, dressed down in a pair of jeans and a T-shirt, but not Natalia. Amelia had learned early on of Natalia's addiction to makeup and heels. She never went anywhere without having her faux lashes attached or stilettos on her stems, and she never allowed the film crew to catch her barefaced. Natalia getting her makeup done was a good start.

"I'm sorry!" the young artist cried.

Natalia reached for a napkin from the makeup-covered vanity in front of her and shooed her away before turning her attention back to Amelia. "Don't worry," she said, smiling sweetly. "How about you go take a break while I talk to my friend here? You can let the cameramen know I'm almost ready."

Amelia leaned forward, her mouth gaping in disbelief. Natalia Ruiz lived up to every stereotype of being a diva. Amelia didn't take her crap, which probably made them such close friends, but others quaked when Natalia was upset. "What happened at your dinner to bring out this softer side in you?"

"Whatever." Natalia rolled her eyes and waited until the doors closed, leaving them alone. "All right fine. Is your mic on?"

"No," Amelia said with a sigh. "Have you forgotten? I'm suspended."

"Suspended?"

"A strongly suggested vacation to take care of my grandmother, same thing." Amelia shrugged her shoulders.

"Wait." Natalia's eyes widened. "For how long?"

"A month."

Natalia's mouth gaped open. "I'm so sorry."

"Don't be." Amelia waved off the apology and forced a toothy smile across her face. "I get to spend some time with my grandmother."

"When I couldn't find you Friday morning to explain—" Natalia patted Amelia's shoulder "—you were still upset about getting the call about your grandmother. It's horrible. How is she now?"

With a sigh, Amelia updated Natalia with what had gone wrong. Grandmamma had fallen down the stairs of her two-story farmhouse down in Southwood. She lived so far out in the country it was a miracle someone had found her. She'd lain on the floor with a broken leg until Pastor Rivers had stopped by randomly—thank God—to check on her on Thursday evening. Amelia couldn't imagine how painful it must've been for her elderly grandmother to come tumbling down the stairs. As a child, she herself had found the stairs too steep for her little legs and had loved sliding down the banister as a shortcut.

"A broken leg," Amelia concluded. "My mama wants the downstairs office for her to live in so she won't have to climb the stairs."

"Is your mom going to move back home?"

Amelia frowned and shook her head. "No way. My grandmamma's home is nothing like your mansion."

"What?" Natalia asked with a pout.

"She has a barn attached to the side of her home, but that's the extent of privacy. Nothing like your place where your whole family lives under the same roof, but you guys can go days without running into one another."

"The grass isn't always greener," Natalia said, glancing down at her hands in her lap.

"I like my privacy, Natalia. I grew up in Southwood, a pretty much one-streetlight town. Everyone knows everyone."

"Sounds cozy."

"Not when you're the one person everyone hates."

Natalia glanced up, her features softened. "What?"

"Never mind. Look, I have a month to get everything ready. Mr. Kelly said as soon as I take care of things back home, I can come back to work. I am going to get the porch steps lowered or put a ramp in there. Grandmamma will have a fit either way, so while she's recuperating in the hospital, I'll take this time to go down South for repairs."

"Good thing MET hosts a bunch of remodeling shows," said Natalia. "You can get any of those guys to fix up the place for free. Hell, you should even turn it into a show."

"We've been spending too much time together," Amelia said with a grin, rubbing her hands on the front of her dark-wash denim jeans, "trying to find the television angle for everything."

"Well, I have to come up with something. I am afraid to ask, but is this my fault?" Natalia pouted her glossy bottom lip again.

Although her friend was wearing so much makeup, Amelia chewed her naked bottom lip. Normally she brushed her lashes a few times with black mascara and maybe a colored, flavored lip gloss and called it a day. "Sweetie, it is," Amelia said dryly. Then Natalia's frown deepened and Amelia let her off with a half smile and a slight push against her shoulder. "I'm kidding."

"I'm so sorry about your grandmother."

"You're not to blame for what happened to her or what happened with my job," Amelia sniffed, pushing the pity party out of her head. Christopher claimed he wanted Amelia to use her hours upon hours of leave time wisely. Just as she'd proven herself in the past to be a dedicated employee at MET, family meant everything to him. Mr. Kelly made it clear for her to enjoy her time with her family and to not be distracted by anything at work. Amelia was prohibited from contacting anyone from the network, so the idea of having help was null and void. Southwood was small enough she could find someone to assist, provided she was allowed to tell her folks what had happened. But Grandmamma wanted to keep the incident a secret. Amelia inhaled deeply. "I am to blame. You were my responsibility."

"But still," Natalia whined. "I do apologize."

Amelia liked to think of herself as a forgiving kind of gal. "Make it up to me by telling me who this mystery man is?"

A part of Amelia wished she had gotten the conversation on film. When Natalia's aunt, Yadira, had approached MET about getting the network involved with their lives, Natalia had already turned eighteen. So there wasn't much that was known of her teen years.

"Stephen and I go back, way back," Natalia explained as her heavy lashes fluttered dreamily. "He's an ex who is practically Villa San Juan royalty. I was glad when his brother contacted me and said he needed to talk," Natalia moaned.

"What happened?"

"Let's just say if *Tía* Yadira had the ability to arrange a marriage, it would have been between us."

"A marriage made in Puerto Rican heaven," Amelia teased as her eyes glazed over, imagining the ratings they would have received. This would have been a perfect angle for a reality show for MET. A multicultural wedding was right up their alley. She pictured in her mind the memo she'd have written:

> *Dear MET executives,*
> *We've watched her grow up; now let's follow the road to the Ruiz wedding.*
> *Sincerely,*
> *Amelia*

"Hey, didn't a mass school shooting happen there about ten years ago?" Other than the tragic ending to a school year, Amelia had heard nothing but good things about Villa San Juan, the small island off the coast of Florida. It was on her lists of places to visit once she gathered some vacation time. Maybe once she made sure Grandmamma was okay, she'd check it out and come back to MET with a follow-up story on the tragedy. For a moment Amelia's eyes glazed over. She wondered if anyone had done a follow-up story. Where were the students now? Had they gotten over the trauma?

"Thirteen years ago, and it was right after Stephen graduated, but his brother and cousins were affected by it. As for me and Stephen, clearly, things did not end well with us, and so I supposed he somehow blamed me for his mistrust in women." Natalia went on about her relationship with Stephen while Amelia made a mental list of who to contact for a follow-up report.

"Oh, sure," said Amelia, her voice elevated with sarcasm. "You'd never do anything to hurt a man's feelings."

Natalia rolled her eyes. "Whatever. Stephen happened before I became famous." She added air quotes with her French-manicured hands.

"Well, don't you have that effect on people," said Amelia. "I've been producing you for a while now and you do have a way with leading men on for your own entertainment."

"Speaking of leading men on," Natalia said, blatantly averting the subject, "I may have told you I was taking a nap, but how did things turn out for you and Nate?"

As if a needle scratched an album off a record player, Amelia's thoughts screeched to a halt. She cocked her head to the side as her heart slammed against her chest and the image of the one-night-stand hottie filtered through her head. Quickly, visions of the night she'd met Nate began to play like a movie on a screen. The ending became all too clear now. The only reason she'd gone down to the bar instead of hanging out with the film crew was because she'd given everyone the night off since Natalia had said she was going to bed. Amelia had gone downstairs to get a well-earned drink.

After years of following Natalia around, Amelia knew when the girl blurted out more than she wanted, especially when she pressed her glossy lips together as if to stop further words. To make things more obvious, Natalia clamped her hands over her mouth.

"I never said anything about *who* I was with." Amelia raised a brow and crossed her legs in preparation of an interrogation. The gold flowers on her flip-flops caught the lighting in the room.

"Okay, fine," Natalia huffed. "Nate Reyes met you on purpose. He knew I needed to speak with Stephen alone. I knew it would be impossible because of the crew but he helped me out."

A sickening feel gurgled in the pit of Amelia's stomach. The room became hot. The five-bulb vanity-mirror lights began to heat her face. "It was a setup?"

"No!" Natalia said, apparently panicking. "I mean. He was just distracting you for a minute."

He'd ended up with a lot more than conversation over a drink. Amelia swallowed past the bile in the back of her throat. *Nate used her.* She glanced at her reflection in the mirror. Always around the glamorous Natalia, she might come off a bit of a plain Jane, but when Nate had picked her up in the bar, she'd felt like the star. Everyone in the bar, men and women alike, had stood taller at the sight of him. And now to learn he'd distracted her on purpose? The whole thing had been engineered. Because of him, she'd been suspended from her job. He needed to pay.

"So he's from Villa San Juan, you say?"

Now Natalia cocked her head to the side as she spoke. "Actually, it's kind of funny you mentioned your hometown. I swear he mentioned living in a Southwood but he never described it as drab as you have. Must be a different one."

"Georgia?" Her mind recalled Nate asking her about her Southern upbringing and how he liked farms. *Turned him on*, didn't he say?

"Yeah, but don't take it too seriously if he flirted with you and bought you a drink," said Natalia.

"Of course not," Amelia mused. Her mind calculated how far her family's farmhouse was from the downtown Southwood. Not far at all, she thought. Perhaps while taking care of Grandmamma, she'd pay him a visit.

"This is going to bug me. Let me find my emails." Natalia reached for her phone in her pocket and began swiping across the screen, mumbling as she searched her listings. "Nate is a big ol' flirt. He didn't mean any harm, but as a matter of fact, I think his playboy ways are about to catch up with the green-eyed god. Oh, look! Southwood is saved in my searches. This is your hometown, right?"

Amelia leaned forward to read the location: Southwood, Georgia, population six thousand. She nodded.

"Cool," said Natalia. "Look, he's up for a bachelor auction. Karma is going to catch up with him because I am sure he's got a handful of women down there. All his women are going to try and cash in."

Seemed like the visit would be sooner than expected. For once Amelia couldn't wait to get back to Southwood—population six thousand, or about to be five-thousand-nine-hundred-ninety-nine.

Despite wearing a black tailored suit, a green Oxford shirt and argyle tie with various blends of green, Nate had never felt more naked than on the night of the bachelor auction. Women groped his pecs, his biceps, and he swore one of the church ladies pinched his butt.

The nightlife at the usual watering hole in Southwood had come out with a roaring blast. The community seemed to have pulled together for this charity event and crawled out of the woodworks at Southern Charm.

Who would purposely come up with the idea of a bachelor auction? If Nate didn't know any better, he'd swear his brother had, just to piss him off. Some of the bachelors he met backstage were already set to be purchased by their wives. Briefly, Nate wondered if the wives did it just to ensure the tasks around their homes would be taken care of. Another part of Nate wondered if the women he'd spent time with in the last few months had gotten together to test his rule of *No complications*. With Southwood being such a small town, Nate understood gossip happened, but he always made sure he never gave the wrong impression. Maybe some of the women felt forty hours of time together could dissuade him. Thank God Pastor Rivers warned everyone about the sin of premarital sex. Nate wasn't usually a religious man, but it was good to know his boundaries.

"Remember, this is for a good cause," Lexi whispered,

nudging her shoulder against Nate's as he waited at the bar for the bartender to return with his longneck bottle of beer.

"I keep telling myself the same thing," he said with a sigh.

The DJ in the elevated booth next to the stage put on a new song, which drafted a lot of ladies to the dance floor. Tonight's event had brought out the old and the young alike. Four-top tables draped in white linen and centered around a single candle circled the dance floor and the second level. A dozen or so silver catering trays showed off some of the traditional hot hors d'oeuvres. He'd peeked earlier and found sweet corn cupcakes, fried green tomatoes, pimento cheese sandwiches and a few trays of deviled eggs sprinkled with smoked paprika. Nate had grown up on traditional Puerto Rican cuisine, which meant a lot of *sofrito*, pork, rice and beans. He enjoyed Southern meals—perhaps a little too much. Thank God for Southwood's gym.

He looked around. He was at a bar filled with women and yet not one appealed to him. Ever since the night he'd met that beauty from Atlanta he'd found no woman who could compare to her. He figured he must be going crazy, because prior to the Atlanta trip, drinking and morally loose ladies were his thing.

His eyes scanned the room for a glimpse of his brother, who'd nominated him for the auction. The bastard hadn't shown up yet.

"Stephen's finishing up some work in his office," Lexi said, reading his mind.

Nate half nodded. "Have you taken a look at the work I did on yours?"

Lexi beamed. "I have! You're fantastic!"

"And cheap labor, too," he joked. For the past few weeks he'd been helping Lexi extend her dress shop. Guilt stemming from the way his brother had treated her when the two of them first met had swayed Nate's decision to help. Thanks to Stephen's spiteful impulse buy, Grits and Glam Gowns and Reyes Realty and Contracting were next-door neighbors. Lexi had been making a pitch for expansion the day Stephen barged into her office.

"I am going to pay you," Lexi said.

"Whatever. I am having fun. Since Stephen decided to move down here, he's contracted many plantation-style homes in southern Georgia to all of Hollywood. And, of course, the kids are getting ready to go back to school. Like my brother said the other day, business is slow. I have nothing but free time on my hands."

The bartender appeared with a longneck bottle of beer and a tumbler of cognac. Nate's eyes darted downward. "I didn't order this."

"The lady at the end of the bar did."

Nate craned his neck, hoping excitedly for some crazy reason to find Amelia Marlow standing there. He grabbed the top of the bottle with two fingers and sipped while glancing down the end of the bar. He prayed he masked his disappointment well. Brittany Foley offered him a wide, toothy grin, swinging her shoulders suggestively to the techno music pounding away. Through each white laser beam flashing through the air, Brittany winked and licked her lips. *The tongue.* Nate willed his body to respond to her nonverbal invitation. *When the hell did he need to will himself?* Brittany's body rivaled all the covers of every swimsuit magazine out there, but in order to keep her job she needed to wear dowdy drab sweaters and long pants and quite often wore her hair up. Away from school, she was a complete knockout. The other men standing around her saw her for the siren she aimed to be.

"You have an admirer." Lexi nudged his shoulder again.

"Don't remind me."

"I thought you two were getting along great at the end of the summer?" Lexi said, casting a glance at the end of the bar. "Philly says you two went out on a few dates."

Nate half grinned. "Yeah, well, Philly is five years old."

"Five going on eighteen," mumbled Lexi. "So what's the deal with you two?"

"No deal." Nate shrugged.

"Will you bring her to the Keaton wedding?"

"Hell no!" Nate all but shrieked. At Lexi's bemused smirk he explained, "She's in a different place than I am."

"Meaning she wants you in her bedroom?"

"Meaning," Nate said with a sigh, trying to come up with what he meant, "she wants things I'm not sure I can provide."

The word *bedroom* only conjured up the image of Amelia Marlow. In retrospect, he did have her phone number and knew how to take the first step. Beside him Lexi pretended to sway. Her fruity pink drink sloshed onto the bar top.

"Nathaniel Reyes does not have the right stuff to give a woman?"

The other women lingering around the two of them began gawking at him with their brows raised. "Keep your voice down."

"Oh, yeah," she said teasing, "we don't want the bidding ladies to think the merchandise is broken."

Nate fought against the impulse to cover his groin as all eyes went toward his lower half. "Will you keep your voice down?"

"Oh, trust me, I don't think anything will stop a bidding war. As a matter of fact, I heard some of the ladies in the church choir comment on how they've pooled their money together and are going to divide up your weeklong stay amongst them."

"What did your future fiancé get me into?"

"A sleazy way to do a good cause," Lexi joked.

Nate turned to her and grabbed her arm. "You've got to do me a favor. Lexi, I need you to bid on me."

"I didn't bring any cash." Lexi stretched her eyes wide with such surprise, Nate believed her.

"I will give you everything in my wallet." Nate reached for his back pocket but a heavy hand patted his arm down. He turned in time to see his smug big brother grinning.

"You're not trying to get my lady to buy you?" Stephen asked, siding up to Lexi with a protective arm around her waist. "You wouldn't want to start any rumors, would you?"

Tight-lipped, Nate shook his head back and forth. Lexi had spent most of her life dealing with rumors about herself, her family and her brother-in-law. Being born a blonde to a family of brunettes was enough to get the townspeople talking. The former beauty queen had had to deal with vicious lies about relationships and of course the clincher—when she left the pageant world and her parents turned their backs on her. Nate admired Lexi. "Funny, considering you're the one who—"

"Another round for my brother!" Stephen interjected himself verbally and physically. He tapped the top of the bar for attention, probably to avoid Nate bringing up the unfortunate topic of how he'd met Lexi. "What are you drinking? Beer or cognac?"

"He ordered a beer," Lexi said, saddling up to Stephen, "but Philly's teacher down there sent this drink over."

Kill me now, Nate thought.

Amused, Stephen saluted Brittany down at the other end of the bar. "A potential buyer? Nate, dance with the woman so she can see what she might be getting."

"Man, in a minute I'm leaving this place."

"You can't go now," Lexi wailed. "Think of the children."

"I'm rich, Lexi," Nate countered with a cocky smile. "I will write a check for a sizable amount."

Another hand snaked around his free arm. Nate turned to the side and flashed a grin at Donna Jean, secretary of the First Baptist Church. She took notes for the pastor and all the board meetings, but in the bedroom, she loved to give dictation. He bent close to give her a side hug.

"You're not thinking about backing out?" Donna said with a wicked grin. Her long nails slipped under his jacket and drew circles down the center of his back. "I emptied my savings account."

"Donna Jean!" Lexi gasped.

"What? I know what I'm getting and I'm not about to let this one slip through my fingers." Donna Jean's note-taking fingers slipped down to pinch his bottom.

Nate tried not to make an obvious gesture to get out of the way. He chuckled and drained his beer. "Well, if you all will excuse me, I think I'll go check out my competition."

Never before had he felt so much like a piece of meat. As he made his way toward the stage, women reached out to whisper in his ears how much money they were willing to spend in order to buy him. If only he had someone he trusted to make the purchase. Too bad a majority of the women in attendance tonight had already sampled a bit of him. It appeared as if every woman he'd told about his no-commitment rule was willing to accept forty hours of his time.

As if to make matters worse, Stephen slapped him on the tail before Nate entered the lionesses' den and shouted, "No competition here, little brother."

Chapter 3

Amelia Marlow smoothed her fingers across the white cloth of her table. The siren-red nail polish matched the body-hugging dress she wore for tonight's activities. Earlier today she had driven east of Four Points to Black Wolf Creek to get a quick mani-pedi before heading off to the bachelor auction. Natalia had offered to make things up to her by getting her pampered for the day, but Amelia did not want to overdo her appearance for her return to the South. Not too many folks would be happy to see her.

Thanks to a high school exposé on peach farmers, Amelia had accidentally, yet singlehandedly, destroyed the town's income. Her intentions came from a good place. She'd wanted to show how her town, and other parts of Four Points, were all connected. Most of the townsmen in Four Points were migrant workers from Southwood, Peachville, Black Wolf Creek and Samaritan. They all worked on the farms for cheap wages, being illegal migrants. Amelia had ended up uncovering a deeper secret about the most of the farmers' tax evasions. Workers were deported and without their help farms had struggled to harvest their crops, then family businesses had perished. Her exposé had had a trickle-down effect, and everyone in Southwood with a peach orchard farm had suffered. Because she felt so horrible for her part in the demise of the town, Amelia never wanted to come back. Instead of wallowing in her guilt, she avoided reunions like the plague and let her love of exposés propel her into studying journalism in college.

The salon in Black Wolf Creek had done an excellent job styling her shoulder-length hair. Her dark tresses flipped off her shoulders, bared in her red strapless body-hugging dress. In her four-inch heels, she was like a panther out on the prowl. Her eyes scanned the tops of the heads of the patrons at tonight's bachelor auction. Her elevated view gave her the ideal spot to prey on the man of the hour. As expected, a crowd of women followed him wherever he went. The corners of her lips tugged downward, as she realized she, too, was part of the admiring crowd. The man certainly knew how to fill out a suit. A close-cropped black beard covered the square jaw she'd stroked during their lovemaking. The palms of her fingers tingled with desire to touch its texture.

The tall single white candle in the center of their table flickered when Amelia's cousin as well as best friend, Cayla Marlow-Beaumont, bumped the table with her hip when she returned with two glasses of red wine. Amelia took her eyes off the bar where Nate stood as the center of attention.

"Thank you," Amelia said, circling her finger around the rim of her glass. "I didn't want to risk being seen."

"Is the dating world this hard?" asked Cayla.

Amelia pressed her lips together and frowned. "This is not about dating. This is about revenge. Nate Reyes used me."

"From what you told me, you used him, too," Cay reminded her. "You left without giving him your information."

Why did she always tell her cousin everything? Cay lived vicariously through Amelia and in return acted as Amelia's conscience. "Information he *clearly* had since he stalked me at the bar and seduced me in order to distract me from my job."

Across the table Cay rolled her eyes. "You're really going to go through with this?"

"I kid you not. Angels sang when Pastor Rivers announced the charity event."

Cay squinted her hazel eyes. "Somehow I do not think you understand what the word charity means."

Amelia's eyes widened with surprise. "Are you kidding me? I donate all the time."

"So you'll donate your time and services for next month's Hardware Hottie Bachelorette Auction?"

"What?" Amelia frowned.

"Kind of like this, but women are auctioning their time. Greg is threatening to nominate me," Cay said with a giggle. "I might need to do some sexy lingerie shopping. Pastor Rivers's guilt speech does not apply to husbands and wives."

Giving her cousin the side-eye, Amelia shook her head. Tonight's event offered forty hours of service from these handymen. The time put in could mean a couple hours of community service here and there. Amelia planned on cashing in her winnings this week. Once she got her grandmamma settled, she was out of here. So any sort

of volunteering of her time was out of the question—
especially not in this area.

"No, thanks." Amelia's frown deepened. "Besides, I am
dropping enough cash tonight that all the schools in four
counties should name a gym after me." As she spoke, her
cousin shook her head, not convinced of Amelia's pledge.
"What?"

"You can afford to hire someone else to fix Grandmamma's place."

"*Principle*, Cayla, *principle*." Amelia cut her eyes back
down to the bar where one woman blatantly ran her hands
underneath the hem of his jacket. If everything went according to plan tonight, she'd prefer to not have him man-
handled and cluttered with cheap perfume. He actually
had the nerve to stand at the bar and pretended to push
off one woman's hand. "Nate Reyes used his wealth and
connections to influence my job and get me suspended."

"Did he *make* you turn your cell phone off?"

"It wasn't off," Amelia confessed before biting the corner of her lip to withhold the wanton grin spreading across
her face. "More like underneath a pile of clothes." Under
the techno lights, she felt her face warm with the memory
of her behavior. With each bright beam striking across her
face, she feared her blush would be exposed.

"See," Cay said, her frown turning up into a grin, "this
is the point where I am going to change the subject." Her
eyes wandered around the open floor space while Amelia
cut her eyes toward her cousin's no-nonsense black slacks,
white collared shirt and Great-Grandma Marlow's pearls.
Far be it for Amelia to judge. Standing next to the Ruiz
family she screamed frumpy, but her cousin—six months
older than Amelia—took the cake tonight. Cay's idea of
dressing to kill meant something completely different; her
attempt to dress sexy tonight could not have gone more

wrong, if Amelia said so herself. When Amelia had arrived at her house, Cayla had met her on the porch before her three children realized Auntie Amelia was in town. With no children of her own or nieces or nephews, Amelia looked at Cay's kids as hers, which went along with the right to spoil them.

"I can't believe we're here again," Amelia said, looking around once they found their table at the club. Southern Charm had been around for years. As a rebellious child, she and her high school friends had snuck into the bar with fake ID's and drank warm beer. The establishment back in the day barely ID'd kids, as long as you were with someone you knew or you slipped the bouncers a few bucks. One of the first shows Amelia pitched was called *Faking It*. The show hadn't taken off because every audience targeted had thought she meant something else, like sexual struggles some women faced in the bedroom.

Nowadays, security was tight and the entry fee to get in was astounding, though tonight's auction didn't make things better. To drag her cousin away from her boring couch with the husband she'd married directly after high school had cost Amelia an extra hundred bucks just to come to tonight's event. She could have possibly shown her credentials from the network, if William hadn't insisted on Amelia leaving them in the Orlando office. A badge from MET was like having a golden key to every event. Everyone wanted to be on television. All Amelia needed was to suggest her new ideas for reality shows and the floodgates opened. Family members told lifelong secrets and the most interesting part of her job was capturing people's behavior when a camera was on them.

The lights dimmed and Amelia sipped on her wine with her auction paddle in her hand. Not letting anyone in on her profession might be the smartest thing she could do.

The way all the women groped Nate, word might spread around, and their behavior might become more blatantly obnoxious. Somewhere in the amount of time Amelia took to look her cousin in the eyes while they spoke, Nate's tall, dark head had disappeared. Women lined the foot of the stage in anticipation, much like singles did at a wedding waiting to catch the bouquet.

Amelia sneered at the desperation and the gall of these women. This bid was hers. For one whole week, the purchased bachelors would do the bidding of the buyer. Everyone else probably had their bachelor in mind and had planned all sorts of sexual events. From the brochure handed out at the door, a few of the men appeared to be married. Amelia didn't think a wife would allow some other woman to buy her husband for the week. She knew good and well the wife would be in the front of the crowd.

The music died down as a handsome man in a black tuxedo stepped onto the stage. The lights in the large club turned off except for the circular bright light on the emcee. Sir Mix-a-Lot's "Baby Got Back" beat pounded off the walls as the deep, rich baritone voice of the emcee spoke into the silver-capped microphone.

"Ladies and ladies," he yelled into the microphone. "I cannot tell you what a thrill it is to find all of you here tonight on a Saturday evening, when there are thousands of other places you could be."

Another noise pierced the room and a light flashed down on the DJ who leaned in closer to clear his throat. "What?"

Laughter bubbled through the crowd. The emcee stood corrected and nodded his head. "Ah, yes, where else would we find such fine ladies but at our lovely Southern Charm?"

The self-promotion received a few catcalls and some

bold shouts from a woman in the back, urging the emcee to get on with the show in a colorful yet vulgar way.

"Well, without keeping you ladies waiting, let's start with bachelor number one."

Bachelor number one strutted out onto the stage, now covered with a red carpet, in a pair of black fireman's boots, suspenders and a jacket, no shirt. He could have been carved from rich dark chocolate. Not surprisingly, women hollered, but judging from the only woman at the front of the pack holding her paddle in the air, Amelia guessed the sexy fireman was her husband. Knowledge of marital rights didn't stop the catcalls. He went for a hundred dollars.

The next bachelor on the stage, whether he was a real policeman or not, clearly was not married. The woman at the table next to Amelia's began fanning her paddle so fast the Brazilian blowout Amelia had gotten earlier today began to poof. A brief bidding war got the amount up to five hundred dollars.

Overall, each bachelor chosen went for a high price. A lot of them Amelia found very tasty, but her paddle was ready for one bachelor and one bachelor only. The emcee teased the audience of women when after an hour of sexy men walking back and forth he began to close the auction down, thanking everyone for coming. For a moment Amelia feared there might a riot of unsatisfied women. Boos and hisses erupted, and there was even the noise of a broken bottle.

"Ladies, ladies, please." The auctioneer patted the air in attempt to calm the crowd. "I'm kidding. I believe we have one final bachelor of the night. He's a bit shy, so put your hands together. Let's welcome Mr. Nate Reyes to the stage."

Amelia gripped her paddle and almost came out of her

seat when the spotlight shined down on what was most definitely the man of the hour.

He tried to keep his expression cool as hell, but deep down inside Nate dreaded the next few moments. An hour ago he'd wanted the right person to buy him so he wouldn't be forced into being a weeklong sex slave. Now, after seeing how much money the crowd had spent on the men before him, he worried everyone had used up their money. The emcee, a deacon from one of the local churches, oversold him with flattering and inflated adjectives.

The acoustics behind the black curtain emphasized the cheering of the women out front, causing difficulties when they tried to hear everything the emcee said. Four of the nearing principals gave Nate the thumbs-up as they pulled either side of the curtain. Salt-N-Pepa's "What a Man" pumped through the man-size speakers to his left and his right. The single spotlight momentarily blinded him. He refused to take a step forward for fear he'd fall off the stage; instead he stood stock-still with his hands folded in front of him. For some reason, no movement at all caused a bigger ruckus.

"Clearly this man needs no introduction," the emcee joked. "Coming from Berkeley Lakes, Georgia, in case you've been living with your head in the sand for the last eight months, this Latino lover is Southwood's newest resident. Judging from the applause, there might not be any need for him to walk the stage."

"Get out here and take it off!" a woman yelled.

Nate bit the inside of his cheek to keep from laughing. The voice belonged to Lexi.

"Hey, now, we're not that kind of establishment," said the emcee. "Can I start the bidding at one hundred?"

Nate bowed his head and gulped.

"Two hundred," another woman shouted.

Before the emcee asked if he could get another fifty, another woman shouted out, "Three hundred." Backstage, he'd heard the new dance instructor went for a thousand dollars. The dancer at least brought his skills to the table. What was he supposed to do with a woman for a week? The ladies around here understood his position; he was an uncle first.

"Four hundred."

"Five hundred."

White paddles with black numbers began to wave in the air, battling the brightness of the spotlight. Nate lifted his head, accepting the cool breeze.

"We have five hundred," announced the emcee. "Wonder what we'd get if he took a few steps forward. Let's see if one of Southwood's newest members can walk that walk."

On cue, Nate stepped forward. In the back of his mind he reminded himself of the good cause. He walked to the left of the stage and caught a glimpse of one of the pageant moms from Philly's class and offered her a wink. The women in the distance all assumed the wink was for them and caused another cool breeze with their paddles.

"Seven hundred?"

"Eight hundred."

Great. Now he was up in the dancer's range. He moved to the right side of the stage and unbuttoned his jacket, driving up the price to a cool grand. When he tossed his jacket over his forearm and loosened his tie, he garnered more catcalls, whistles and a two-thousand dollar bid. Nate had watched enough of Philly's pageants to understand how to work a crowd. He moved to the front and center of the stage.

"I've got two thousand. Do I hear a—" the emcee began.

"Twenty-two hundred."

A bidding war began in four different directions of the downstairs dance floor. Heads bobbed from the left to the right like at a tennis match as the price went up with every wave of the paddle. Nate caught the voice of one woman, a mom from Philly's pageant team. This same woman had pushed her hotel key card in his hand and whispered her child's nap schedule. The other woman's bidding came from the bar and Nate was pretty sure it was Brittany. She came from money, plenty of it. Did he need to guess what she wanted from him for a week? The bidding between the two women slowed down as the price went to five thousand dollars. A lot of *ooh*s and *aah*s filled the room. Their shouts to outbid each other were crisp and angry.

"I hear five thousand. Do I hear fifty-one hundred?"

All eyes turned toward the pageant mom. Her kid needed braces soon. She pressed her lips together and gave her head a quick shake.

The emcee continued his countdown to close the bid. "That's five thousand going once."

Nate pictured himself swiveling on the round bed in Brittany's dominatrix bedroom. He'd been to her two-bedroom apartment downtown, but he'd never been led back to the second bedroom with the padlocked door. Once she'd run into the room to get some more condoms and Nate had spied a lot of leather, whips and chains. As sex-crazed as he could be, that was not his scene. The thought of being held captive sent a faint ache to his wrist. Or she'd want something worse—for him to take her to the Keaton wedding as his plus-one.

Nate didn't do monogamous relationships but he also did not lead women on. Taking a woman to a wedding was a gateway to commitments and complications. Nate didn't have time for either.

"Ten thousand dollars!"

The emcee dropped the gavel on the podium and let out a few words of shock. "I'm sorry, ma'am. Did we hear correctly?"

The voice came from the second level. Nate glanced upward but his eyes watered under the light. He lifted his free hand to block it in an attempt to check out the highest bidder. Red dress, curves for days, the swell of ample breasts, luscious red lips which curved into a devilish smile. Nate's pulse began to race realizing he knew the body—biblically. Another spotlight flashed on Amelia, making them the only two in the room. He gave a prayer in thanks that he'd remembered to loosen his tie because he almost could not swallow.

"Ten thousand dollars going once," the emcee counted. "Going twice. Sold to the lady in red," he cheered and banged his gavel down.

An uncomfortable silence pierced the night club. Someone cleared their throat and someone dropped their keys. From the bar Stephen and Lexi stood up straight and began clapping their hands over their heads. A slow, reluctant applause broke out from the crowd, all remembering tonight's cause.

The emcee leaned into the microphone once more. "Four Points, thank you for your generous donation. Might we learn the name of our benefactor?"

From the stage Nate finally noticed the other woman with Amelia. She rose from her seat and leaned across the banister. "Her name is Amelia Marlow."

"Amelia?" the emcee repeated. "Oh, snap, one of Southwood High's own?"

Amelia lifted her arm in the air without smiling. Nate's brow rose to meet her...*glare*? An icy chill crept down his spine. On many given occasions, Nate had pissed a woman off and had resorted to feigning cluelessness. He recognized the look she gave him—he recognized it well—but this time, he didn't deserve it. She left him at the hotel with no notification that she wanted to see him again.

"Well, ladies and gentlemen," the emcee announced, "this concludes our evening for real this time. We'd like to thank you once again for your generous donations this evening from all our ladies, as well as our participating bachelors. Feel free to stay around and enjoy some drinks and we hope to see you next week."

Nate turned to exit the stage with his mind still wondering what bothered Amelia. A round of applause greeted Nate backstage in the dressing room area. He made his way against the men who'd already changed out of their outfits and were about to meet their parties. All he wanted to do was get into something more comfortable and meet Amelia outside, preferably in his car on the way to her place. The sooner they started this weeklong venture, the better. Where did she live? One of the Four Points? Forty hours was not going to be enough time.

To no surprise, the ringleader started off the slow clap. Due to present company, Nate refrained from flipping his brother the middle finger. "Stephen, what are you doing back here?"

"I came to congratulate you, little brother." Stephen clapped his hand on Nate's back. "I knew those green eyes of yours would bring in top dollar."

"You're my pimp now?"

"Hey." Stephen shrugged and laughed. "You're the one out there with the ladies about to fight."

"Only one winner tonight, though," teased the fireman who'd gone first.

Nate threw his black jacket down on the bench by the locker containing his favorite jeans and T-shirt. He considered tossing his overnight bag into the back of his SUV and leave wearing his slacks and shirt.

"She may have won tonight." A female's voice penetrated the room.

The men still dressing in the backstage area covered their modesty as Brittany waltzed through the room, her eyes boring holes in Nate's. Shirt on but unbuttoned, he still felt naked. Nate shrugged his shoulders, trying to indicate his indifference, but she kept coming toward him.

"And this is my cue to leave." Stephen bailed on his brother. "Miss Brittany, I trust Philly and I will see you on open house night at the school?"

"Perhaps." Brittany gave Stephen a sweet smile, warranting a whistle from a few of the guys. Nate shot a glare around the room, not as protection but to dissuade any encouragement. Brittany did not need to leave here thinking there was hope for them. She just needed to leave—period.

One by one the men began to leave, allowing them privacy. Nate had no desire to deal with Brittany tonight. His pulse raced with the idea of being with Amelia. Still, she stalked closer, one black-heeled foot in front of the other in a straight line, licking her mauve-tinted lips.

"The forty hours you have to put in doesn't mean in a row," she purred, stopping her pointed heels in front of his shoes. "You can work ten straight hours each day and then in four days I can have you all to myself."

"But judging from the busy workload you presented at Philly's orientation, I am sure you'll be too tired." Nate ducked his head to the side before she attempted to kiss him. The only lips he wanted were Amelia's. "We can catch up next week at the school."

"There's always the Keaton wedding."

Hell no, he thought.

"I'm not sure I can wait that long, *papi*."

Nate tried not to cringe at her fetish nickname for him. He certainly wasn't her daddy. "I need to get going."

"Oh, yes." The corners of Brittany's mouth turned upside down. "To meet Amelia Marlow. How did the two of you even meet? You know we went to school together. I thought she'd never have the nerve to step foot in Southwood ever again."

He couldn't miss the disdain in her voice but he tucked it away to question Amelia over dinner one night this week.

"Tell her, Nate," said a voice from the back door.

Brittany spun around and stiffened against Nate's body. The wisps of her hair against his face made him want to sneeze. Amelia Marlow leaned against the door with a slight grin and a raised brow. Her long, slender arms folded across her chest, just under the swell of her breast. Nate's mouth went dry, while the rest of his body went into full-blown adolescent desire.

"This isn't what it looks like," Nate blurted out, gently pushing Brittany's shoulders off him to step out from behind her. In four long strides, he crossed the room to embrace Amelia, but her scowl stopped him from proceeding.

"You don't have to explain a damn thing to her," Brittany growled.

Nate ignored the schoolteacher and embraced Amelia, well aware of the stiffness of her body. "Darling, I cannot express to you how glad I am to see you again."

"Afraid you exhausted all your connections in Hollywood to find me again?"

Sarcasm dripped from her red lips. His eyes widened. The gig was up. His mouth opened but no words formed. Perhaps now was not the time to confess he'd gone straight to the star herself for the information on Amelia.

"Close your mouth, dear," Amelia sneered. "For the

record, your stunt got me fired and now I'm going to lose my apartment."

The left corner of her luscious mouth twitched. Nate licked his lips to refrain from grinning. She'd done the same thing their night together when she said she needed to leave after round one. "Fired, you say? Are you sure it was wise to invest your money in me?"

"I have a use for you."

"I had a feeling you'd be back for more," Nate said, baring his teeth and leaning forward. "But you didn't have to pay a dime."

The pulse against Amelia's neck quickened against his tongue. Nate grinned into the kiss he planted against the curve of her neck. She tasted as sweet as he remembered—maple-y. He could eat her right here and now. But Brittany's irritating foot stamp and annoying sigh reminded him they weren't alone. Nate pulled his face away but not before capturing her bottom lip between his lips. Amelia mewed a slight moan. Whatever ailed her, he knew how to fix. Without thinking, Nate reached for Amelia's thigh. The hem of her dress tickled against his fingers as they snaked for a touch of her petal-soft skin.

For a brief moment Amelia seemed to relax against his body. She turned her face away from his kiss and winced as if in anticipation of his touch. Again Nate grinned, but this time he blew out a breath of relief knowing he still had her. His laugh killed the moment, as did the sudden straightening of her back and the slap across his face. Nate touched his burning cheek and watched Amelia storm out. In his other hand, he realized, she'd somehow pressed the address where she was staying. Things were beginning to get interesting.

Chapter 4

Nate turned his SUV onto the gravel driveway off County Road Seventeen. Before tearing out of the parking lot he followed the closest car speeding away and took the chance that Amelia was the only one leaving the party early. Judging from a half glance at the address given to him, this was the place she wanted to meet him.

The tires crunched across the pebbles. The pulse at his wrists twitched against the black leather steering wheel as his eyes focused on Amelia's shapely legs swinging out of her vehicle with the rented tags. The silhouette of his headlights caught the angle of her feet in her spiked heels. As his body stiffened, he was reminded to go ahead and turn off the engine and unbuckle his seat belt. So focused was he on getting to Amelia that he'd forgotten to take his keys out of the ignition when he opened his door. The sharp dinging reminder echoed against the side of the barn attached by a breezeway to the two-story home.

Amelia stood to her full height at the driver's side. The interior light of her car shone on hips encased in her red dress. He'd never loved a color so much. He couldn't wait to rip the material from her body. Nate stepped out and stalked toward her. Gravel scraped the bottom of his black dress shoes. A defiant smile spread across her face when he neared her body. Women did not challenge him. He loved this prelude to a proverbial dance they were about to do. Nate closed her driver's-side door behind her, pinning her against it.

"What are you doing here?"

"Getting a start on whatever it is you want me to do to you." The light in her car died off, leaving them alone in the night air. An owl hooted off in the distance over the sound of a diesel truck entering one of the back roads. With all the nighttime orchestra, Nate still heard her gulp, not in fear but uncertainty. Had she bitten off more than she could chew by bidding on him tonight?

"Are you going to tell me what you have in store for me now?" Nate asked. His eyes focused on her plump lips. She'd reapplied a layer of gloss during the ride over here because he knew he'd kissed off the strawberry flavor back at the club.

"In a rush to get back to Brittany?" Amelia countered. She pressed her manicured hand against his chest in a seeming attempt to put some space between them, but he felt the way her fingers lingered against his pecs.

Nate cocked his head to the side to study her face for a moment under the half-moon's light. "Babe, you've got me for a full week."

"And then?"

He grinned. "Planning on keeping me around longer than the forty hours?"

The light caught the slight red tint to her high cheekbones. "Already narrowing the amount of time you have to spend with me?"

"You paid for forty hours." Nate dropped one hand from the car and traced the length of her left arm with his fore-finger. "I'm staying for a week, 24/7."

"When you see what I've planned for you—" she licked her lips and batted her lashes "—you'll want the break in between."

"Now you're talking." Nate lowered his face to hers; his lips hovered near hers as he breathed in the distinct, fresh strawberry scent. Her breast lifted forward with a deep breath of anticipation of a kiss; he decided at the last moment to not give in. It wasn't just the lingering sting on his cheek telling him something was bothering her. She held him responsible for her getting suspended and he needed to fix this. It took all his might to tear himself away from her, but he pushed away from the car and took a step to the right. "But first we need to talk."

Had he not been standing there so acutely aware of her body, he may have missed the way she slightly leaned forward. She caught herself and pressed her backside against her door, hiding her hands behind her tail. "What?"

"Is this your suitcase?" Nate asked, peering into her backseat. Before getting an answer, he opened the door and took the black canvas bag out. "All right, where are we headed?"

He moved toward the walkway to the house. Where the driveway was gravel, a cemented walkway provided a sturdier pathway to the large wooden steps of the front porch. Earlier when he pulled into the driveway, he thought he spied a rocking chair when his lights flashed on the house, but found a set of four instead. For some reason he imagined a younger version of Amelia shelling peas into a pot as a child. In his career as a real estate agent and contractor, Nate had an eye for homes, especially ones that told a story. Even in the dark, he knew this was a colonial plantation house; the wide porch and tall pillars clued him in. He couldn't wait to get inside. Speaking of which, he realized Amelia was slowly walking up behind him. Why so shy now?

"Don't tell me you're worried about spending the night with me," he asked with a teasing grin.

"I'm not," Amelia said, standing at the bottom step, "because you're not staying in the house with me."

"Excuse me?" The house was so far out, it was too damn late to drive back to Southwood now and not wake the girls when he got home.

"Well, I'm staying in the house—" Amelia pressed her hand against her breast "—but you're staying there." Her manicured hand pointed toward the barn.

"I'm sorry, what?"

"The barn. I hired you to work forty hours for me."

Nate dropped the bag and leaned against a white pillar. "So I'm here as your farmhand?"

"I figured it's only fair."

"I don't get it." Nate walked down the steps until they were face-to-face.

As if to distance herself, Amelia folded her arms across her chest. "Don't play me for a fool, Nate. Not again."

He cringed.

"Yeah, I talked to Natalia. I'm not just a field producer, Nate, I'm also her friend. You knew exactly what you were doing when you bought me that drink last week."

"Amelia," he tried.

"Save it." She hushed him with a wave of her hand before securing herself against the frame. "I was a fool to ever have a drink with you and a bigger fool to bring you back to my room. You wanted me distracted? Well, you got it. I was so distracted, as you planned, that I didn't get the footage of Natalia and your brother talking."

"They needed privacy."

"She signed a contract to have her life videoed 24/7," she said, "thus making me miss an important turning point in the show."

Nate shook his head. "I'm sorry you feel that way, but my brother's life is not part of the show."

"Well, neither is mine now."

"You were seriously fired over missing one conversation?"

Amelia rolled her eyes before biting the bottom corner of her lip. "I'm here, aren't I?"

"Well, tell me why I'm here."

"Like I said, you will be my farmhand here for a week. My grandmother had an accident and you're going to help me."

So revenge was on her mind? Nate's eyes narrowed down on hers. "You do realize these forty hours are causing me to miss my nieces' first day at school on Monday."

"Well, looks like we're both missing out on important benchmarks in our lives. Good night, Nate Reyes."

Thanks to the sound of someone's rooster serenading him at the crack of dawn, Nate woke up a few hours earlier than he was used to over the summer. The beat of his heart settled when a shadow of the feathered friend walked past the thin crack between the wooden panels of the barn. At least the door to the breezeway remained closed. He didn't want to start the day losing any cool points by tangoing with the thing. God only knew if Amelia had rigged the barn with hidden cameras just to enjoy the torture. Wasn't it her profession to capture every moment of someone's life on television? His eyes peered left and right and in all the corners of the barn. A small camera could fit somewhere in the rafters or in the bales of hay. Shouldn't he see a red light flashing if he was being filmed? None captured his attention.

With a groan he rose from the lumpy, plaid, orange-and-brown couch he'd slept on and stretched, feeling every bit of his twenty-eight years. To be kind, the old double-crib barn was cozy. These buildings housed livestock back in the day but the latest trend was to convert these two-story structures into livable spaces to rent out for extra cash. Last night had not gone according to plan, at least not Nate's plan. The old army blanket and sheets folded on top of the glass coffee table indicated the night had gone as planned for Amelia. Her idea of revenge was buying him for forty hours of what? Community service? For a chance to be with her again, *he* would have paid.

The pressure of the springs against his back relieved once he rolled his head from side to side until a crack sounded off. A water heater set up in one of the corners of the barn cranked to life, flushing water from the pipes. Outside the dusty window of the barn, Nate spied a light coming from a rectangular window upstairs. He moved from the couch to the window.

In an unfair torture treatment, Amelia's naked frame crossed by the window. She had to be unaware of the view she gave him. In the reflection of the mirror, a perfectly shaped breast bounced as she fingered her strands of hair underneath a pink shower cap. As she stood in front of the mirror, making sure none of her strands were exposed, Nate enjoyed the image of her heart-shaped behind facing him. His fingers tingled with the memory of her delicate, soft skin against his rough hands. One caress of her skin soothed him to the bone. Speaking of, Nate glanced down at himself and shook his head at the uncontrollable desire she evoked from him with the distant observation. He couldn't recall the last time his body responded to a woman without her touching him. And given the cold shoulder she'd presented to him last night, touching him seemed to be the last thing on Amelia's mind.

Nate considered ducking from the window when Amelia turned from the mirror, but realized she couldn't see him being a peeper. Once the reflection of the daisy-patterned shower curtain moved, steam stained the mirror.

A breeze blew from the screen door of the breezeway. The scent of strong coffee flowed from the open window in the house next door. Nate rolled his head around on his neck and tried to recite the starting lineup for the Miami Marlins to take his mind off the adolescent effect of Amelia's nudity. Once he was able to walk straight, he grabbed his Timberland boots, jeans and red-and-white striped shirt before heading off toward the scent. Nate always kept a spare change of clothes in his gym bag in the trunk of his car on the occasions he needed to spend the night elsewhere.

Like the barn, the breezeway seemed to have become a storage space for old things. The screen siding of the outdoor hallway did not seem like a wise place for an old juke box or records. Southwood wasn't too far away from the Florida border and still received torrential downpours of rain during the hurricane season. Whatever Amelia had planned for him, he made a mental note to move the equipment to a drier space.

Four steps led up to the kitchen door. A small, square doggy door flapped as he opened the door. If the size of the pooch door gave any indication, there wouldn't be a monster inside waiting to eat him for entering unannounced. But then again, didn't the pot of coffee brewing on the marbled countertop seem welcoming? A circular table sat with the leaf side against the wall for more space in the kitchen. The wood flooring appeared to be in good shape, not creaking when he stepped farther inside. A significant amount of care had gone in to the wooden cabinets. Brass knobs new and shiny. A blacktop gas stove matched the specks in the marble counters. Two red mugs sat upside down in the sink; he grabbed both and wiped them off with the red-and-white dishcloth hanging from the door handle of the black refrigerator.

The first sip of coffee was always Nate's favorite, the first jolt of caffeine flowing over his lips. *She made a mean brew*, he thought with a twinge of a smile. After his first few sips he moseyed over to the table and picked up the top of the envelopes on the table. In the state of the table, the condition of the breezeway and the rickety shape of the furniture, Nate half expected to find a red stamp with "past due" on the front of the envelope. There was none; just a lot of bills for Helen Marlow.

"What do you think you're doing?"

Nate glanced up and grinned at the sight of Amelia standing at the entrance of the kitchen. Her bare feet teetered against the plush beige carpet and the hardwood floors. Her toes were painted red, different from the French manicure he'd kissed not too long ago.

"Helping myself to a cup of coffee," he answered and moved back toward the pot. "I set aside a mug for you but I realized I didn't know how you like yours. Had you not left the hotel room last week, I might have learned what you liked—coffee-wise, that is."

Amelia's hand closed the slight opening of her yellow bathrobe. Water trickled down her shapely legs and her hair was now free of the shower cap. Dare he mention what he saw?

"You got what you wanted that night."

Since he had no reason to lie, Nate nodded his head. "I did get a lot more than what I wanted, Amelia. I never intended for you to get fired. Natalia assured me she was able to get private time after hours."

"Whatever." Amelia shook her head. "I don't have time to rehash the past."

"A week ago was the past?" Nate half laughed.

"In my world you're old news."

Ouch. He managed not to wince at her harsh words. Growing up in Villa San Juan with his first cousins, Marisol and Lourdes, he'd seen firsthand how ruthless women could be when hurt. "Okay, I'm old news. What kind of headlines can I make for you today? You have me all to yourself for a week."

"Forty hours."

Nate nodded. "I stand corrected. Do you have a time clock you'd like me to punch?"

"I'd like to punch something," Amelia mumbled, turning her head toward the living room.

"We did something similar—" Nate refrained from continuing the millisecond Amelia cut her eyes in his direction. He held his free hand in the air in surrender. "All right, let me stop."

"Thank you."

"Why don't you tell me what you want me to do?"

Amelia sighed and shrugged. Her arms dropped to her side and her shoulders slumped as she inclined her head toward the stack of envelopes on the table. "This is my grandmother's place. Last week, the phone call I received right after we—" her cheeks tinted a faint pink "—well, my grandmother took a spill last week and broke her leg."

"A spill?" he repeated.

"She fell down the steps." Amelia pointed her thumb

over her shoulder to where he guessed the stairs were. "And she broke her leg."

Nate raked his left hand through his hair. "Geez, I'm sorry."

For a split second Amelia softened and smiled. "What happened to my grandmamma isn't your fault."

"But," he said with a nod, "what happened with your job is." The silence falling between them gave him his answer. "All right, so what is it you want me to do?"

"She'll be home this week and I want to move everything around, but I'd like to start with a ramp on the side of the porch and then we can work our way inside."

Nate's brows rose with amusement. She rolled her eyes and clarified, "I'm talking about moving all of her things downstairs into the office space."

"Is this what she wants?"

"It's what I want."

"Then your command is my wish," Nate said with a bow.

Thank God for strong pillars. Amelia, dressed in a pair of gray yoga pants, her favorite University of Alabama shirt and red flip-flops, leaned against the cool, large column and took in the vision of sculpted muscle. Sweat dripped down the center of Nate's back. He stood with his back turned from the house for a break, resting his elbow on the top of the shovel. It was already noon and in three hours he'd prepared a space behind Grandmamma's hydrangea bushes for a hidden ramp. Nate briefly argued that her grandmamma did not need to advertise her age nor her ailment if she was going to be the only one living here by herself.

Without knowing, Nate's words caused Amelia to cringe inside. Every time she spoke with her mother, she was riddled with guilt, maybe survivor's remorse. She'd left town and never looked back, but would anyone blame her? Southwood was a small step up from Mayberry and Amelia had bigger plans for her life than being the wife of some peach farmer. Perhaps at one point in her life she'd thought she would live in town, run her family's ice-cream parlor and live happily-ever-after, but everything had changed when everyone in town had turned on her family. *So much for small-town loyalty*, she thought with the bitter tug of a half grin. According to everyone, her article for the paper hurt businesses.

A drizzle of cold moisture trickled down her fingers from the glass of iced tea she held. Amelia shook her head to shake out the unwanted memories. The square ice cubes clinked against the glass, and Nate turned around. Amelia's heart seized against her ribs when he smiled. Sunlight glinted in his dark green eyes. His mouth opened for a bright, toothy smile and his bicep flexed when he waved at the sight of her. Dark hairs sprinkled against his chiseled jaw from missing his morning shave—she refused to feel guilty about that. Amelia turned her glare from his, spying the crumpled up T-shirt he'd stripped out of on the gravel driveway. The man needed to be on camera. If she were a casting agent, she'd place him as the heartthrob, the one who would go on to be a star. If Nate could get her insides all gooey, she could only imagine what the rest of America would do at the sight of him. Hell, last night his lingering kiss had crept into her dreams. By the time she woke up, she'd needed a nice cold shower.

"How's it going in there?" Nate called out.

Despite the giant glass of ice tea she'd polished off in the kitchen, Amelia's mouth went dry. Did her desire for him read across her face? Damn it! In her world of highly emotional women and situations, she practiced constraint on her desires. One bat of an eyelash from one cast member at another could spark an entire storyboard and carry the show throughout the season. The summer heat cast a layer of moisture across her forehead and in the palms of her hands. The glass slipped and the ice clinked again.

"What?"

"Inside." Nate pulled off the familiar brown work gloves from the barn. "You were moving some of your grandmother's belongings from downstairs?"

"Oh, um…" Amelia fumbled for the words to say as heat crept up her neck. "Yes, I'm making headway."

To say "some of her belongings" was an understatement. Amelia did not want her grandmother risking her life again by tripping down or up the steps, but she herself had nearly tripped a few times bringing some of Grandmamma's church dresses downstairs. She knew her grandmother would have a fit when she came home—but this was for the best.

"Is that for me?"

Amelia followed Nate's head nod toward the glass in her hand. She held her breath as Nate climbed over the trellis onto the side of the porch. With each step he took closer to her, her heart raced. With one hand he reached for the glass, while with the other outstretched hand he held out a couple of long-stemmed daisies. She loved the simple flower. Nothing said being in the country like stretching out on a bed of daisies, gazing into the sky and guessing the shapes of clouds. As he took the glass, their fingers grazed against each other. Sparks emerged. To recover from them, Amelia dropped her hands to her side, and the petals brushed against her thigh.

"So kind of you to allow your ward a sweet tea break," he said after a long sip. His profile of his lips against the glass could start a whole new ad campaign for tea.

"We're in the South," Amelia said with a frown. "It's just tea."

"My sister-in-law says the same thing."

"Who?" Of course he came from a family; the man wasn't truly sculpted and created by God and placed on earth to torment women.

"Well, future sister-in-law?" Nate took another long sip. "Any day now my brother is going to propose."

Amelia's spine stiffened with the memory of why she had mandatory vacation time. "Did your brother have to get a ring back from Natalia?"

"Cute." Nate squinted his green eyes toward her. Under the cover of the porch's roof, their color darkened. She wondered who he inherited them from. Light brown or hazel eyes ran in her family but had skipped her. "If you don't know the story, you're getting nada from me. And don't assume all men fall for Natalia."

"What's that supposed to mean?"

"Not all guys go for the glamour." Nate stepped forward to close the gap between them. He braced his empty hand against the pillar right over her head. "Some guys like a woman who doesn't need all the makeup and lashes."

Conscious of her lack of face paint, Amelia tucked a stray hair behind her ear, forgetting the flower in her hand. Nate reached down and helped her with the stem, then tucked it behind her ear. A breeze blew into the narrow space between them, pushing her Alabama T-shirt away from her bare breasts. Had she been in the spotlight of one of her shows, a camera would have panned in on the way her nipples hardened. God forbid if Nate thought he was the cause.

"What do you think you're doing?" Amelia asked.

"I thought we were having a moment." Nate dropped his hand to his side. "No?"

"We had our moment."

Amelia straightened her lips and prayed her eyes did not give away how much she wanted him to kiss her right now. They had thirty-seven more hours left together and she wanted to make the most of this time together. Any man who carried around a spare change of clothes in the trunk of his car was not the commitment type. Forty hours might be his longest relationship. A wasp in the corner of the ceiling caught her attention. His eyes followed hers, then tore away from the nest. A shiver ran down her spine.

"Are we on hidden camera?" Nate asked.

Eyes narrowing, Amelia's upper lip curled on the left side. "What?"

"You're in the reality TV business," he said as if that explained everything.

"Was." Amelia inhaled and glanced around at the blue hydrangeas blooming. Her arms folded under her breast, creating distance—again. Why did Nate always seem to corner her off? She could move, but he was the one who brought his behind over here.

"So there are no cameras on this property?"

"What?"

Nate stepped back and half sneered, half laughed. "Come on, Amelia. You make a living out of filming other people. Maybe you're tired of them being the star."

"And I suppose I am making you my costar?"

The lopsided grin he gave her sent a shiver along her arms. "You can't deny we'd make a fabulous flick. Want to try?"

"Go find Brittany Foley for your freaky stuff." Amelia frowned. The words irritated her. She and Brittany had never seen eye to eye even before Amelia's article. Amelia did not buy the goody-two-shoes act from the pastor's granddaughter. In high school, Brittany made no secret of the fact that she had been not just more active but more advanced in the bedroom than the rest of the girls.

"Cute." Nate stepped back. A dribble of sweat rolled down the center of his bare chest, over the ridges of his perfect abs and disappeared into the waistband of his black boxer briefs. His hung just slightly low, allowing for the vision of his V-shaped muscles. A spasm shot to every pressure point of her body. A low seductive laugh broke her out of her daze. When she glanced up, Nate's eyes followed hers. "Well," he began, breaking through the crackling tension between them, "let me get back to the work at hand." He stepped toward the stairs and paused by her shoulder. "That is what you brought me here for, right?"

"Of course." Amelia jumped away from his body. "What else?"

Nate nodded his head. "Just asking."

Amelia waited until she heard the shovel going back to work against the Earth's dirt before she went back inside. The minute she entered the doorway, she went straight to the pitcher of iced tea and poured the beverage down her shirt.

Chapter 5

"You changed."

Nate's baritone voice startled Amelia as she daydreamed at the kitchen sink. For a while she'd found herself kneeling against the armrest of the flowered couch in Grandmamma's sitting room and staring out the window, crudely watching Nate's body in motion. Bulging biceps flexed when he shoved the shovel into the ground. His back muscles rippled as he turned to throw the dirt off to the side of the trench he built. When a tad bit of drool actually touched her bottom lip, she had decided to stop torturing herself by ogling his body.

"I got a little wet," Amelia explained, and when he raised a quizzical dark brow she shook her head to shake off the embarrassing heat creeping up from her neck. "You're a pervert."

Funny, she'd called him one when she was two seconds away from grabbing her battery-operated friend while she watched him work outside. Nate leaned against the wall of the entrance to the kitchen. He must have found his way through the breezeway. Disappointedly he'd covered up with his T-shirt back on.

"I came in here to see if you had any more tea."

Embarrassed by her wantonness, Amelia cut her eyes toward the pitcher brewing on the ledge on the windowsill in the late-afternoon sun. The darkness of the amber liquid indicated it was done. She reached for its red handle. "Sure."

Nate pulled out the chair closest to her and turned it around, straddling it as she pressed one of the glasses she'd washed against the ice-dispensing compartment of the refrigerator. Even with her back to him, she knew his eyes were all over her body. Why had she chosen the short denims? Did it really have anything to do with the ninety-nine-degree weather outside? Or did she subtly want to seduce him as he worked?

"When does your grandmother get out of the hospital?" he asked.

Amelia pressed the glass against his hand and let go quickly so their fingers didn't touch. Good thing his fingers were so large they brushed against hers. "In a few days. But if she keeps getting on the doctors' nerves, sooner."

One of the nurses had left a text message for Amelia, informing her they were considering allowing Grandmamma to finish her rehabilitation at the house. She'd wanted to know if Amelia had the house ready yet. Technically everything upstairs was now set up downstairs, as far as clothes went. Amelia needed to take out the couch and bring in a new bed. After Amelia left, Cay would be able to take care of the daily errands for their grandmother.

A dimple appeared in his right cheek when he grinned.

"I think I have an idea. I have a grandmother who is pretty spunky myself."

"Do you?"

"Yes, *Abuela* Caridad." Nate's smile went from seductive to boyish at the thought of his family. "She would kill me if I moved things around in her house."

Barefoot, Amelia stepped backward to lean against the sink. "Does your *abuela* live by herself twenty miles away from civilization—" Amelia snorted "—if you call Southwood civilization?"

"Hey—" Nate feigned a frown "—don't knock my town."

"Your town?"

"Yeah." He leaned forward on the two back legs of the chair. "This place is great." His left brow rose. "And there's more than one streetlight."

"Barely," Amelia mumbled, remembering when she gave him the description. A jolt of excitement shocked her system. "I guess Brittany has made Southern living pretty comfy for you." *If ever she could eat her own words.*

"Brittany has been very accommodating," said Nate. A sudden desire to wipe the smirk off his face washed over her. The tingling sensation in her fingers overwhelmed her, so she folded her arms beneath her breast.

Amelia hated the unfamiliar green streak rumbling through her veins. She'd captured it before in the editing room after going through footage. She knew that when a bulging vein crept out of the middle of someone's forehead or jaws clenched together, the green-eyed monster was getting ready to enter. Film-wise, capturing the moment was gold. Personally, Amelia wanted to crawl under the table and die. Then, like verbal diarrhea, the snide comments couldn't stop. "I bet she has."

"Brittany understands the deal."

The deal? What was the deal and why did it make Amelia want to scratch Brittany's eyes out? Amelia did not do those things. Sure, she'd aired a lot of catfights, but she herself did not partake in violence. "What is your *deal*?" She hated herself for asking.

"I don't do complicated," he said, reaching behind him to set the now-empty glass on the table.

"Oh." She relaxed her lower back. "I understand."

"Do you?"

"You don't like attachments. I don't, either."

Nate's luscious lips pressed together. Did her use of the term bother him? "When was the last time you dated someone?"

One of the perks a field producer had was asking questions. Back in the day, she'd cut her teeth on a reality show, meaning she'd worked in a house filled with a half dozen highly volatile young ladies, where she and a crew had filmed everyone for six days straight in order to obtain enough drama to produce a thirty-minute episode. One might think having a minor in psychology was a waste of time in this business, but Amelia used hers as a skill to evoke emotions. She took what she saw on film to question problematic situations, whether there or not. Every confessional she edited raised the most drama on reunion shows. In the scheme of things, Amelia understood what buttons to push. This was her job. Not Nate's. "Let's talk about something else."

Amused, Nate shook his head from side to side. "Nah, what's wrong with answering the question?"

"Because I know where this will go," she said with a sigh. "I'll answer your question and then I'll ask you the same."

His mouth spread into an even more amused grin.

His golden brown arms folded over the back of the chair. "Okay. I have nothing to hide from you."

"Because I already know when your last relationship was." Amelia pressed her finger to her chin, pretending to ponder the question. "Um, or shall I say relations?"

A cloud covered the late-afternoon sun, shading Nate's face. The grandfather clock in the living room chimed five times. On cue, Nate's stomach growled. Come to think of it, she had not offered him breakfast or lunch. Most people working eight hours out of a day deserved a meal.

"It's quitting time," Amelia said.

"Or happy hour," he suggested. "What do you say?"

Laughter escaped her lungs. "I remember the last time I drank with you."

"You say it with such a frown that my ego insists on a do-over." In a quick swoop, Nate lifted his leg over the chair and advanced on her.

With the sink at her backside, Amelia had nowhere to go. The only thing possible was pressing her arms against his chest—his massive, hard chest with muscles that she'd watched flex and glisten in the sun. The memory of the ease with which he'd swooped her into his arms and carried her toward the bed, where he'd feasted on her body, flashed through her mind. Desire pooled between her legs. *Why was she stopping him?*

"Hold on." She found her bearings. "This is not happening."

"Because you want free labor?"

"Because you played me," Amelia corrected.

Nate sealed her against the sink by pressing one hand on either side of her. "I thought I explained myself."

"So? A murderer doesn't get a get-out-of-jail-free card by explaining the way he killed someone."

"You're warped," Nate said with a laugh. "You know that?"

"I've been called worse," Amelia said, shrugging.

The height difference between them without her heels was blatantly obvious when he straightened. Nate belonged on the runway or a basketball court. His thick brows rose with a question.

"Tell me about it over dinner." His voice softened with apparent concern and his hand snaked out to take hers. "Off the clock."

At least at dinner, Nate would be covered. Of course, Nate possessed the ability to make a duffel bag look good. "I don't think so. I don't go out when I'm in town."

"No problem," Nate said cheerfully. "I'll cook."

Fine, gorgeous and he could cook? What could go wrong?

What could go wrong? More like what couldn't go wrong? To say Nate started a full-blown fire was exaggerating. Sure, the flames were high, but the smoke had been the scariest part. And speaking of smoke—where it was, there was fire. At least, the fire now brewed in Nate's system. He was the one with the obsessed thoughts and dreams of Amelia. He refused to let his opportunity to be with her be threatened by someone else. One of Southwood's finest firemen lingered on the porch, talking and flirting with Amelia. He got it; she'd been gone for a while.

"I can't believe you're really here." Fireman Parker Ward was the first to greet Nate in the Marlows' driveway. He introduced himself after assessing any damages, claiming to have been familiar with the address and wanting to personally make sure Helen Marlow was okay. When Amelia stepped out from around the side of the house, the guy had been following her around like a lovesick puppy.

Amelia rubbed her fingers across her chin. She leaned a hip across the railing of the porch. Parker stood too close for Nate's comfort, with his fireman's hat in his hand, coat open and shamelessly displaying the snug T-shirt. Who did he need to write a complaint to? Nate's mind tried to recall the name of one of the bachelors from the auction, but he was too busy eavesdropping from the other side of the door. Was this even professional?

"Well, I can't say I'm here for long, Parker," Amelia said with a slow Southern drawl Nate had become familiar with from the other residents of Southwood. When they'd met at the hotel bar, she'd spoken with no trace of an accent.

Parker nodded. A series of smiles passed between them. "Well. I hope while you're here you'll let me cook you a real dinner."

Seriously, dude? Nate's fists balled. The dig of his fingers against his palm snapped a bit of reality into him. Nate reminded himself he did not do complications. Amelia had made it clear she did not plan on staying in town. Nate loved Southwood and planned to be here for the long haul. He was at the Marlow residence for a job and when that was complete he owed her nothing. Well, at least maybe dinner tonight.

"I'm not sure you cooking me dinner is a good idea."

"I—" Parker pressed his helmet against his chest "—am a great cook. Ask anyone at the station. Besides if anything should catch on fire, I'll put it out myself."

Nate closed his eyes and counted to ten in order to keep from ripping the screen door off and choking the smug fireman. A light, airy giggle sounded off. Realizing he'd never made Amelia giggle without touching her irritated Nate even more. From his angle, he saw Amelia's face light up. The corners of her eyes softened and her smile widened.

"You're still crazy," Amelia replied.

"And you're still beautiful," said Parker. "But of course I may be biased."

No bias, Nate thought. Anyone with a pair of eyes saw the beauty in Amelia. From what he understood, she spent her career filming people when *she* needed to be on film. Now there was something worth turning on the television for.

"Oh, Parker, stop." Amelia flirted on.

Yeah, Parker, stop. Nate rose from the back of the couch, ready to interrupt, when one of the other firemen honked the horn on the truck.

"I've got to go," Parker announced. "But I am serious about catching up with you before you leave. I understand you don't want to run into folks but maybe I'll meet you at FP General for a cup of coffee. It will give me a chance to catch up with Miss Helen. I had no idea she'd hurt herself."

The squeak of the screen door caught their attention. Both Parker and Amelia turned toward him. Amelia's face was more quizzical, while Parker shot him a glance of irritation for the interruption. The man did not care for Nate's presence. *Whatever.* Amelia was his for at least thirty-two more hours, with a bonus for dinner tonight.

After the local fire department cleared out of the driveway, the desire to cook a meal gone, Nate convinced Amelia to let him take her out for dinner. Women didn't resist his invitations to dinner. With Amelia, it seemed more like an act of congress. With people like Donna Jean or Brittany, they wanted to be downtown at one of the local restaurants, depending on the night. Since it was Sunday, most were closed, with the exception of some of the old eateries closer toward the town square, run by families who spanned generations in Southwood. Nate decided to take her choice to eat at a newer pizza joint across town as flattery, and tried to read it as a desire to have him all to herself, but somehow he couldn't fool himself. Amelia did not want to be out with him; that she'd picked the corner in the back of the pizzeria where no one would see them clued him in.

"Did you leave here under WITSEC orders?" Nate teased.

Amelia's dark eyes stopped skimming the laminated menu long enough for her to furrow her brow. "What?"

"You're all cloak and dagger." Nate nodded at the way she held the menu in front of her face. "Unless you need glasses."

The way she frowned was cute. The corners of her mouth turned upside down and her bottom lip poked out. A shoe made direct contact with his shin. "My eyesight is perfect."

"Not just your eyesight." Nate cocked his head to get a glimpse of the hourglass curve of her shape.

"Does your cheesy machismo usually work on women?"

Nate flashed a grin. "It worked on you last week." He regretted the words the second before he finished the *k* in *week*. Amelia's foot came into contact with his shin again. "Sorry. Chalk this up to being nervous."

Amelia settled back against the black leather booth. "You're supposed to be nervous?"

"Who wouldn't be?" Nate relaxed in his seat. "You breeze into town and drop a wad of cash on me just to make me do work for what you could have hired someone else to do, and much more cheaply, too."

The little flower in the center of her white spaghetti-strap top rose up and down. Even through the flicker of the flame bouncing off the deep maroon glass candle holder, he caught the way her cheeks turned pink.

"Let's say I don't trust anyone around town to do the work for me."

He stopped himself from mentioning Parker's name. The man seemed too eager to spend time with Amelia. Clearly, the two of them had history together.

"So you work on a reality show directing all kinds of odd jobs." Nate shrugged and cleared his throat to get the thought of Parker out of his mind. What mattered was that Amelia had declined Parker's offer and accepted his. "Couldn't anyone else do the work?"

The frown disappeared and Amelia glanced around the room. Her teeth captured the bottom corner of her lip. "I am not allowed to contact any of the folks from the shows I produced."

"You're the producer." Nate leaned forward. "That explains the cash flow."

"Was," Amelia clarified, twisting her lips to the side— her reminder that she'd been fired because of him. Nate bowed his head in apology. "And I was a producer, but not in the sense most people think."

"I'm not most people." Nate wiggled his brows.

"I was a field producer, which meant I oversaw a lot of the production. I traveled with at least a dozen guys to keep up with the Ruiz crew, depending on what they had going on during the day." Amelia paused for a moment when the waiter approached with their sodas and a notepad ready, to take their order.

Now raising two kids, Nate rarely ever got to order a pizza with more than pepperoni or cheese on top. They both thought the Supreme sounded delicious. *Kismet yet?* Probably not, but he did find her desirable when she asked if he'd be okay with a deep dish. The waiter disappeared into the kitchen.

Nate reached across the table and captured her hand.

His thumb stroked small circles on the bones of the back of her hand. "You were saying?"

"About the pizza?"

"About being a big-time producer."

Amelia's eyes lit up with excitement. "Field producer."

Nate chuckled and inclined his head. "Okay, what is a field producer?"

Long lashes fanned against her high cheekbones as she contemplated her answer. Her cinnamon-kissed skin glowed in the light of the camera. A blush shone across her high cheekbones. "What's your favorite reality TV show?"

"Don't have one." Nate rested his arms on the table.

Amelia cocked her head to the side and spoke slowly. "Because you have so many?"

"Because I don't watch them."

Amelia's eyes narrowed and she leaned forward as if she didn't hear correctly. "Pardon me?"

"I don't watch reality shows." Nate's shoulders rose up and down, shrugging as she sat across from him clutching her heart and dramatically feigning being wounded. "I live with my two nieces, and if a show has to bleep out every other word because women are fighting or tearing each other down, it's not worth watching."

"All right." Amelia nodded. "I can understand to an extent. But what about *Azúcar*?"

A tremble threatened to lift his upper lip. "What about it?"

"It is the first crossover American reality show with a predominately Puerto Rican cast. It's my number one project for MET Studios."

"Hey, that's fantastic." Nate tried not to come off sarcastic. "But to me, the Puerto Rican *cast* is plain old regular folk."

"Of course," Amelia groaned and hit her forehead with

the palm of her hand. "I forgot how close you and Natalia are. Exactly why did Stephen and Natalia meet up?"

"I'm afraid if Natalia did not tell you the nature of the meeting," Nate said with a sigh, "then it's not my place to tell. I will say I've known her family for years and I know for a fact they're headed by an egotistical woman named Yadira who sees nothing but dollar signs when it comes to her nieces and nephew."

"Aunt Yadira isn't so bad."

Nate studied Amelia's face as she spoke. Her bottom lip twitched and she glanced away for a second. No one got along with Yadira Ruiz. "Because she's the one padding your pockets," Nate grumbled.

"MET Studios pays my salary," Amelia snapped, "or they did."

The animosity in her voice came in loud and clear. He wanted to hang his head in shame knowing he was the reason she'd lost her job, but she needed to look on the bright side. He'd done her a favor. "The studio is a platform for money and greed."

Amelia sat back, tight-lipped. Her dark brown eyes glanced up to each corner of the ceiling. The huff of breath blew a stray strand of hair that had escaped her ponytail out of her eyes.

"Are you looking around for cameras?"

"No." She sighed. "I'm looking around for places I'd put a camera if I wanted to create a show."

"Habit of yours?" Not sure if he preferred her avoiding eye contact with him or taking the icy glare she gave him now, Nate wiggled his brows.

The bells over the door jingled. The young girl behind the counter shouted out for the new guests to have a seat wherever and let them know someone would be with them in a moment. Meanwhile, the door to the kitchen swung open and a waiter came out with a pizza for another couple. Nate watched Amelia, who'd gone back to observing the restaurant.

"I like to come up with different ideas for shows," Amelia finally answered him, resting her elbows on the table. Out of habit with Philly, Nate moved Amelia's glass of soda out of the way. "It relaxes me. How long have you lived with your nieces?"

"About eight months."

Amelia nodded as if she already knew but tested him. "How old are they?"

"Sixteen and five," he answered.

"How are they doing?" Amelia spread her fingers flat on the table, almost touching his, but as if she was too afraid to make a move.

Nate half smiled. "They're fine. Better than I was when I heard the news."

"It's so noble of you to take care of them."

Nate placed his hands over hers again. "I can honestly say they're the ones taking care of me. Do you have any brothers or sisters?"

"Not really." She rolled her eyes toward the ceiling. "I mean, I have bunch of cousins. One is like a sister to me. Cayla, well, we call her Cay. She was with me last night when I…"

"Staked your claim on me?" Nate chuckled. She tried to withdraw her hands but he held on tightly. "Stop pulling away. I'm not going to hurt you."

"But—" Amelia raised her left brow and offered him a challenging smile "—I don't want to get burned."

Had they not been in a public place, Nate just might have pushed the salt, red pepper and parmesan cheese shakers to the ground and lifted her onto the table. *Hurt her?* He wanted to protect her, cherish her and even worship her body. That was not too complicated, right? "Amelia, you're going to have to learn to trust me. I understand we got off to a rocky start yesterday."

"Because you set me up?"

Nate nodded. "If you want to view it that way, okay. But despite why I needed to see you, understand I wanted to be with you the moment I laid eyes on you. I'm not going to hurt you. Do you believe that, Amelia?" Was he pleading with her? When had he started pleading with women? Each second she took to answer caused a notch of strange insecurity in him. "Do you believe you won't get burned with me?"

"At the moment." Amelia shook her head back and forth.

Dying to know what she meant, Nate leaned forward. Did she believe he'd burn her? Didn't she understand how much he wanted to be with her? "Tell me what I need to do to get back in your good graces?"

"What are you talking about?" Amelia yanked her hand away before he could protest. "I'm talking about the pizza."

"What?" Nate felt his brows furrow.

"Pay attention, the pizza's here."

Chapter 6

With the pizza stand between the two of them empty, Amelia sighed at the thought of their evening ending. Tonight was the first time she'd gone out with no one or nothing hounding her, not her work or her past. Nate made an irresistible dining partner. His humor kept her from jumping every time a car passed by the windows or the bell chimed when the door opened. The last thing she wanted to do was be spotted by someone in town. She wanted a smooth in-and-out when it came time to leave.

"You have to have dessert here," Nate suggested, polishing off the last morsel of pizza crust before wiping his hands on the napkin in his lap.

Unlike most women she knew, Amelia did not act shy when it came to eating in front of a man. The pizza had been layered so beautifully, with fresh mozzarella, paper-thin prosciutto, crispy pepperoni and some of the freshest vegetables around. When their pie arrived, she'd vowed to eat the whole thing, but the buttery parmesan crust had fooled her and she only managed three slices. Dessert seemed out of the question.

"They have the best *affogato*."

"Gelato or ice cream?" Amelia perked up.

Nate's lips pursed together. "You know your desserts?"

"I know my frozen desserts," she replied with a nod. "My folks used to own an ice-cream parlor downtown." A part of her wondered why she'd told him. She hated talking about being from Southwood.

"No kidding?"

"I promise." Amelia crossed her heart with her forefinger and raised her other hand in the air. "The Scoop, off Main Street."

"Original." His nod of approval caused her to beam. "Did your folks retire?"

"They live in the California mountain area of Little Tujunga now," she said, sitting back. Their waiter came over to clear the table and take their dessert order. Having a combination of gelato and coffee didn't sound like it would help her get any sleep tonight and she'd already tossed and turned last night, no thanks to Nate.

Now with a clean table, Nate reached across and held out his hands for her to take. For some strange reason, she did. "Do you get to see your parents often?"

"Good God, no."

"Why do you make it sound crazy?"

"How often do you see your folks?" she countered.

"I saw them for the Fourth of July and I'll see them Labor Day weekend for the Crystal Coquí."

"The what?"

The way Nate shrugged his shoulders, she thought he might be playing down this event. "It's a banquet my family puts on once a year to honor the big business contributors to the community."

"Sounds fancy."

"Tux-and-evening-gown fancy," Nate confirmed. "It is embarrassing."

"Wearing one?"

"The event." The corners of Nate's eyes crinkled. Amelia's stomach did a flip, but she contributed it to the massive heap of whipped cream on the dessert bowl the waiter placed in front of her.

"We should have ordered a small one to share," said Amelia.

"I'm greedy." Nate swiped his spoon across the chocolate shavings on his dessert. "I don't share."

A familiar pang of desire that tugged inside her stomach had her somehow wishing he wasn't talking about the dessert. "You don't have an ounce of fat. I don't know how or when I'm going to work all of this off."

"I'll help you." Nate's eyes now narrowed on her. This time she understood he wasn't talking about the dessert.

Amelia cleared her throat, hoping to keep the heat of the threatening blush from being exposed. "Tell me more about this Crystal Coquí. Why is it embarrassing?"

"I used to think it was more of a way for my family to feel better about themselves."

"Better?" Amelia's inquisitive nature was piqued. Natalia mentioned Nate came from a good family.

"Ah, it's probably my pops talking." He shook his head as if to get the notion out of his mind. Amelia leaned forward, literally on the edge of her seat. She wanted to learn everything about this man. Lord only knew when she'd get a chance to be around someone not in the business again. "Tell me."

"My dad, Esteban Reyes," Nate began after one big

bite, "he always felt he needed to compete with my mom's family, the Torreses."

"Compete how?"

"I guess when you marry into the family whose ancestors discovered the island, there is a bit a pressure."

"Your family *founded* a city?"

By the time Nate finished telling the story about the claim his grandfather many times over had staked on the island, located off the northwest coast of Florida, from the famous explorer Tristán de Luna y Arellano, Amelia was in awe.

The young explorer had tried to establish the Pensacola Bay area but was not successful. Hurricanes defeated many of the ships trying to enter the bay. And when another conquistador, Ángel de Villafañe, came and offered to take the settlers to Cuba, Vincente Torres and a few others stayed behind and were offered the opportunity to stake their claim in any part of land they felt they could tame. Vincente Torres inhabited the island, not far off the coast of Pensacola, and his descendants had already brought over several family members by the time Spain officially founded Pensacola in 1698.

Where the explorer failed, Vincente Torres managed to maintain the island, which had reminded him so much of his beloved city on the nearby island, and would become Puerto Rico; hence the namesake, Villa San Juan. In 1845, Florida became an official state. With Villa San Juan being a part of Florida, all inhabitants became American citizens.

"The wheels in your head are spinning," Nate said with a chuckle.

"Your home sounds fascinating."

He shrugged modestly. "It's a small town, just like Southwood."

Amelia frowned. "There's no history here. Your family *founded* a city."

"Perhaps, but everyone wants a piece of the Torres family, their wealth and their rum. At least in Southwood, everyone comes together as a community. Take the bachelor auction."

The townsfolk of Southwood did come together, even when running a family out, she thought. "Whatever. Didn't your community come together over a school shooting?"

The prideful gleam in Nate's green eyes from when he'd spoken a moment ago disappeared. The thickness of his eyebrows hooded his orbs. A chill ran down Amelia's spine.

"The shooting took place a long time ago. We've all gotten on with our lives."

"Did you know the shooter?"

Nate poured a spoonful of coffee over his gelato, then set it against the ring with a clink. He blew out a sigh—the familiar sound indicating he did not want to talk about what happened.

"Did you leave town because of that?" Amelia inhaled deeply, then pressed her lips together. During confessionals on her reality sets, she always asked the hard questions—the thought-provoking questions, even the emotionally charged questions—and never felt any qualms over doing it.

"Tell me why you left Southwood." Nate turned the conversation back on to her. The deep chuckle eased her mind. "What do you have against it?"

"Where do I start?" Before Amelia got the chance to rattle off a long list, a figure approached their table. Amelia stiffened at the memory of the familiar face.

"It has been killing me all night long," the tall, slender woman said with a friendly smile. "Amelia Marlow, right?"

"Emily Keaton," Amelia acknowledged coolly with a tight-lipped nod. She braced herself for confrontation, squaring her shoulders and sitting back against the vinyl of the booth. What she wasn't prepared for was for the former head cheerleader to bend over and embrace Amelia in a friendly hug. The last time she'd seen the girl, she was making a cheer about Amelia leaving town. Not sure what to do, Amelia patted Emily's back. Over the garlic and fresh bread, Emily smelled like a bouquet of flowers. "Hello."

"What are you doing in town?"

"Family business," Amelia said.

Emily tucked behind her ear a black strand of hair that had come loose when she bent over for a hug. "Please say you'll be in town until Saturday. I'm getting married at the Methodist Church. I'd love for you to come."

"You can't be serious." Amelia jumped when a foot connected with her shin. "Ouch." She glared angrily across the table, only to find an unapologetic smile across Nate's face.

At Amelia's pain Emily turned her attention to Nate. "Oh," she hummed knowingly.

"Emily, this is Nate Reyes." Amelia made introductions.

Instead of extending her hand for a firm shake, Emily leaned over and hugged Nate's shoulders. Of course they knew each other. Was there any woman in town who didn't know Nate?

"Hey, Nate," Emily cooed. "You have to promise me you won't tell Lexi you saw me in here scarfing down some pizza. She'll kill me if I go up a dress size after my final fitting."

Nate cast a glance in Amelia's direction. "I can honestly say my eyes have been on one person all evening." He offered a wink in Amelia's direction. The heat of desire boiled in the pit of her stomach. "Your secret is safe with me."

"Thank God!" Emily turned her attention back to Amelia. "So you'll definitely come now, right? With Nate, he's already going to come, so it'll be fun."

"Yes, come," said Nate with a deep baritone voice. "It will be fun."

The table in the back of the restaurant, the dimly lit candle, the decadent dessert—it dawned on Amelia this situation might be taken the wrong way. Emily thought they were here as a couple. Amelia shook her head quickly from side to side. "Oh, no, this isn't what you think."

Nate reached across the table, covering her hand with his. "Not sure if you heard the story, but Amelia was the highest bidder at last night's bachelor auction."

"Aw," was all Emily said.

Paranoid, Amelia wondered what the "aw" was about. Did Emily find it pathetic that Amelia bought Nate? Did she think the only way she'd get a date was by purchasing one? Amelia surrounded herself on a daily basis with gorgeous, hot men. Hell, after ten years of avoidance, Parker seemed overly eager to spend some time with her. Who wouldn't want to be around her? She was smart, successful, creative and ambitious. And if she did say so, she was pretty damn good-looking, as well. *So why did it bother her what Emily thought?*

"Well, I finally have the name of your plus-one, Nate," Emily said. "I can't believe you're really here, Amelia. We have so much to catch up on."

No, we don't, Amelia thought. "Again, I'm not one hundred percent sure I'll be here by Saturday."

"If you can't make my wedding," Emily said, placing a hand on Amelia's shoulder, "you should at least come to my bachelorette party Friday night. I have a bridal shower during the day, which of course you are welcome to attend. Mama's throwing it, so I cannot say for sure how boring it will be."

The way Emily went on, it was as if she'd forgotten all the drama Amelia had caused with her article. She would have sworn she'd been transported back twenty years and received the itinerary for a sleepover. Amelia wasn't sure if she needed to grab a shovel for this BS or a shovel to dig her own grave if she agreed to attend any of the events.

Not getting her answer, Emily reached down and gave one last hug before excusing herself. "Just think about it. I'm in the book."

"You look shocked," Nate said when they were alone again.

"That Southwood still has phone books?" Amelia commented before picking up her dessert spoon.

"Cute, but you know what I meant. Let's get back to what we were saying before Emily came over here."

"What?" She played innocent, batting her lashes at him.

Nate cleared his throat. "Oh, I believe you were about to rattle off all the problems with Southwood."

Thanks to Emily and all her chatter, the gelato had melted into the coffee. Amelia spooned another bite of the now-extra-sweet coffee. Aware he watched her lips, she curled them over the spoon and licked it clean. "I have my reasons."

"Sure, because everyone is so horrible here? The nerve," he scoffed, "of Emily coming over here and inviting you to her wedding. I can't believe her audacity to invite you to her bachelorette party." Then to make matters worse, Nate sat back in the booth, folded his arms across his chest and pretended to mope.

Weeks after the article, her friends were no longer hanging out with her. Invites to graduation parties were rescinded. Amelia didn't expect Nate to understand the misery a teenage girl felt when she was abandoned by her closest pals. So Amelia did the only thing she could think of and threw the rest of her dessert square in the center of his chest before getting up and leaving.

"You didn't have to drive me to the hospital." Amelia took Nate's gentlemanly hand and allowed him to help her out of the passenger side of his SUV. This was the first they'd spoken since she left him at the table last night. His hooded green eyes dared her to defy the offer of his opened door when she stepped foot onto the porch.

Yesterday afternoon, after she'd listened to the despair in the nurse's voice, Amelia had made plans to see the medical staff and apologize on behalf of her grandmother. When she'd come down from her shower this morning, Nate was in his suit from Saturday night, wrinkled and disheveled. A part of her was surprised to see him turn his SUV into the driveway last night.

As mad as she was at him, she was grateful he'd interrupted an awkward goodbye. With the pizzeria across the street from the fire station, she couldn't help but go over and ask for a ride. Parker, as he'd been when they were teenagers, had been all too willing to come to her aid. Just as they had on her porch earlier, he lingered again for a while, apparently wanting to say a lot more. Amelia's life now did not include having a small-town boyfriend, and having to tell him so again would be just as heartbreaking now as it had been then. Nate's lights in the rearview mirror had saved her from Parker asking her out again.

"Of course I needed to escort you here," Nate said. He closed the door behind her but didn't move, much like the first night he followed her home. "It's the least I could do, since you didn't let me drive you home last night."

"You were being childish." Amelia's pink-and-white polka-dotted ballerina flats hit the pavement of the sidewalk. She tugged at the hem of her white T-shirt-material dress so her thighs didn't show. A string of pink pearls hung around her neck. She wore them for Grandmamma's sake, who insisted no Southern girl should go out without her pearls.

"You're going to blame last night on me?" Nate followed her down the pathway toward the hospital.

Amelia stopped walking. Nate trailed so close he bumped into her when she paused. She spun on her heels and craned her neck to look up at him. "I left this town for a reason. I have nothing but bad memories."

"Your whole life here?"

An Elvis-like curl came over her upper lip. "What does it matter to you if I hate this town or not?"

The front of his shirt expanded with his deep breath. "You're right. My bad. I was thinking, with you being unemployed now, you might want to stay here."

A fluffy cloud blew over the hospital. "Why?"

"Didn't you mention something about losing your apartment?"

Did she? How soon she'd forgotten stretching the truth. She needed to keep a diary to keep track of the things she told Nate. Amelia glanced back at the sky. The cloud had now disappeared. A storm was brewing. "I don't need you to worry about my finances."

Nate threw his hands in the air for surrender. "All right."

They both started walking again. "I don't need you to walk me into the hospital, either."

"I want to make sure you get in safe and sound," Nate said as the automatic doors slid open, but not before Amelia caught a glimpse of his smirk.

A few seconds passed before Amelia's eyes adjusted to

the difference of the lights in the receptionist's area. The young woman smiled in relief at the sight of her.

"Miss Marlow." She snatched off her headset and came around the circular desk to embrace Amelia.

Amelia awkwardly patted the girl on the back. When did Southwood become such a hugging town? However, unless she was crazy, Amelia was sure the girl shuddered. "Is my grandmother okay?"

"She's fine." The girl sniffed and regained her composure. "Miss Helen is actually in the waiting room with a guest."

Being part of the community, Helen Marlow had lots of friends. But she'd wanted this accident to be a secret, so Amelia was curious about who was visiting. She followed the plastered signs toward the waiting room; all the while Nate was on her heels.

"Really, Nate." Amelia inhaled deeply.

"What?" He chuckled and captured her hand. Amelia did not pull away. "Are you afraid to be seen with someone like me?"

They fell into step together. To be honest with herself, Amelia enjoyed facing off with her grandmother with someone by her side…especially someone like Nate. With Amelia being so close to thirty and not married, Grandmamma reminded her constantly.

High-pitched laughter echoed down the hallway. Amelia rounded the corner to the open room filled with dozens of chairs, a few vending machines and a coffeemaker. Two figures sat close together by the window. There was no mistaking Grandmamma's propped-up white cast.

"Grandmamma?"

The gentleman seated with her stood up and crossed the room to meet her. "Well, Amelia Marlow, as I live and breathe."

"Pastor Rivers." Amelia dropped Nate's hand.

"Nate?" Pastor Rivers pulled back from his hug to Amelia. "This part of your community service?"

"Yes, sir." Nate cleared his throat. "Just doing my duty and bringing the young lady to her grandmamma."

"You don't get to call me that." Grandmamma maneuvered her wheelchair around in an awkward circle, knocking several of the folding chairs over. Amelia went to help but her grandmother swatted her hand away. "Who is this you brought here?"

"Grandmamma—" Amelia inhaled deeply "—this is Nathaniel Reyes, but he goes by Nate."

"Well, Nathaniel," Grandmamma said in a clipped tone, "don't you own an iron or is this the new fashion?"

Nate smiled and thankfully ignored her grandmother's gruffness. "It is a pleasure to meet you, Mrs. Marlow. May I say you have a beautiful home?"

"What the hell are you doing in my home? Lord, Amelia, you better not have all kinds of people up in my house."

Somewhere deep inside her, the seventeen-year-old Amelia shrank into herself. "No, ma'am. Nate's been helping me fix things up for you," she interjected before Grandmamma began lecturing them.

"Miss Helen," Pastor Rivers spoke up, "Nate is an honorable young man. I can vouch for him."

Grandmamma glared skeptically at Nate with her hazel eyes. "Well, whatever you two are doing, best get it done soon. The doc says I can finish recuperating in the next day or so."

"Yes, ma'am," said Nate.

The Southern drawl he spoke with turned her on when it shouldn't. Amelia shook the sound of his deep twang out of her head. She preferred men with more of an international range, much like when he had rolled his *R* when they were in bed together. *Mmm, bed together.* Was it getting hot in here? Amelia's fingers itched to fan her face. She hadn't realized she'd been daydreaming as Nate explained what they were doing. When she came into focus, Grandmamma's face was skewed with a frown.

"Think about the good they're doing, Miss Helen," Pastor Rivers said, stepping between Grandmamma and Nate. "They're moving everything downstairs so you won't have to climb those stairs every single night. Won't that be better for you?"

"Tell me about your day, girls." Nate pushed a plate of store-bought cookies in front of his two favorite nieces, who were now pouting. "Did Uncle Stephen get you off to school okay?"

Both girls widened their eyes at him. Philly's mouth opened and she quickly covered her mouth to suppress her gasp. "Girls?"

Kimber folded her arms across her sparkled T-shirt. Her smirk, so much like her father's, made him grin. With Stephen in town to help on a more permanent basis, Nate was able to enjoy more grown-up activity apart from the house. The love he had for the girls, however, never allowed him to spend more than a night or two away. He'd spent two nights away with Amelia—sort of. He'd still slept on the couch in the barn last night.

"I believe you did not use the correct pronunciation in my name," said Stephen, coming down the kitchen stairs.

"Oh." Nate laughed. "Did *Tío* Stephen get you off to school on time?"

"Why would you ask them such a question?" asked Stephen. He opened the fridge and grabbed the gallon-sized milk container.

"Uh, because the last time you were supposed to take

the girls to school, you overslept and they stayed home for the day."

"Not all of us." Stephen cut his eyes at their oldest niece.

Kimber blinked her lashes innocently the same way Amelia had last night. "School was fine, *Tío* Nate."

"Miss Brittany has more paperwork for you," Philly said, shoveling a chocolate chip cookie in her mouth. "She said you should come by after school today."

The back of his jaw twitched as he ground his molars together. Brittany should not be passing messages on through his niece. "What? I spent all last week filling everything out. You can handle it this time," Nate said to his brother.

"But she loves it when you work with her." Stephen set the milk on the table and pinched Nate's cheeks. Nate swatted his hand away. "She might be the only person in the world willing to put up with you and your wrinkly ass."

"Oooooh," Philly exhaled. She sat on her knees to try and pour a cup of milk without everyone helping. Nate cringed at the idea of milk spilling everywhere, but she did it without making a mess. Did she learn this while he was gone? Why didn't Stephen text him and let him know?

"Girls, thank *Tío* Stephen for funding our trip to *Abuela*'s next week," said Nate. He rested his arms on the table and spun the cold jug around.

"Ugh," Kimber moaned. "Labor Day can't get here soon enough. I need a break."

Nate shook his head. "I thought you said school was great."

"Yes, I did. I saw my old friends and made new ones. I had to listen all day to everyone's wonderful summer stories, the summer I wasted because you two grounded me."

Nate pretended to be really interested in what Kimber said, resting his face in his hand and nodding when she went on about how her evil uncles had grounded her all because they did not understand her. "Tell me more."

When Kimber realized he was making fun of her, she stormed off, Philly in tow. Stephen took the opportunity to sit in one of the unoccupied chairs and dig into the cookies. The plastic container crackled with his meaty hands cramming inside. "So what's really going on?"

"What do you mean?"

"I haven't seen you since Saturday and I almost put out an APB on you."

Half smiling and half nodding, Nate chuckled. "I am okay. I needed to stop in and grab my contracting contacts. And some clothes." He wasn't sure why he added the latter.

"So the auction girl is working you hard, huh?"

"Don't read too much into it," Nate groaned. "Amelia is more about revenge and the chick is taking her anger out on me."

"What did you do?"

"Distracted her, and by doing so, made her mess up a work duty."

Stephen ran a hand over his bald head. "What am I missing here?"

"The auction chick worked with Natalia."

"Oh, her producer?"

"Field producer," Nate said with authority, now that he'd learned more about the reality television world.

Cookie crumbs fell from Stephen's beard when he pressed his lips together. "Hmm," he hummed. "You guys are getting close."

"She's prickly, but I'm getting through to her. I'm going to help her get her grandmother's place fixed up. You ought to meet her."

"The girl or the grandmother?"

"The grandmother. She's pricklier than Caridad. And

her attitude…" Nate went on. "Last night she threw her dessert at me, and this is after I agreed with Emily about her coming to Saturday's wedding."

"The grandmother?"

Nate shook his head, his eyes half closed. "What?"

"Who are you taking to the wedding?"

"Amelia," Nate replied, a breath away from adding, "Duh."

"You know what all this sounds like to me, Nate?"

"What?"

"Sounds complicated," Stephen commented with a raised brow.

Stephen's words resonated in Nate's head the whole drive back to Four Points General. He didn't understand how things were complicated. Amelia blamed him for the destruction of her life and he felt the need to set things right for her. Without a job or probably now any income, she needed to establish her life in Southwood. Whatever had happened here for her, he was sure could be fixed.

The smell of antiseptic snapped Nate out of his daze. A candy striper greeted him at the front desk after he walked in through the sliding glass doors. "Hi, I was here a little while ago with my, uh, friend, Amelia Marlow. She's here visiting her grandmother."

"They're in the cafeteria." The young girl pointed in the opposite direction from the waiting room. "If you need me to walk you down, I'm more than willing."

Nate offered a wink to the girl, who couldn't be much older than Kimber. "I've got this, thanks."

The soles of his tan Timberlands squeaked against the linoleum floor. At least the yellow caution sign near a bucket made him aware of the need to slow his pace. He did so and began walking to the beat of his heart—quick.

Why did his heart skip a beat with the anticipation of seeing Amelia again?

The soft laugh he'd heard her make floated into the corridor. Nate wondered what her grandmother had said to cause such a genuine sound. An image popped into his head of the two of them sitting on the porch in one of the rocking chairs, sipping on some iced tea and Amelia laughing at something witty he'd say. Light spilled into the hallway at the entrance. The smells of stale coffee mixed with some probably unsalted chicken breasts and plain rice filtered in the air. The closer he got, the more the scent of the food overpowered that of the cleaning materials.

He stopped at the entrance, letting his eyes find the Marlow party. People—patients and doctors—filled the large room. The tables were square and colorful in shades of pale turquoise, pink, green and yellow. In the back of the room, a line formed in front of a dinging cash register. The laughter sounded off and Nate narrowed his glance toward the back of the room. Amelia faced the doorway. Her hand clutched her pearls and her head dipped back at whatever someone was saying to her. The sun shone against her dark hair and haloed her head like an angel's.

"Damn, you clean up good."

Nate had been so caught up on Amelia, he hadn't noticed Helen Marlow being wheeled up to him by a girl favoring Amelia in looks. Amelia had mentioned she came to the auction with a cousin. Because she met him backstage, Nate never met the relative face-to-face. The similarities were uncanny. This must be her.

"Grandmamma," the girl who wasn't Amelia scolded, giving a shake to the rubber handles of the arms of the wheelchair. "Don't embarrass the man."

Pressing his hand on his chest, Nate glanced down to inspect his attire—denims and a fresh white V-neck T-shirt.

"Don't be too hard on her. This is a step up from what I wore earlier."

"Well, on her behalf, I'm sorry." She leaned forward and extended her hand. "Please to meet you, Mr. Reyes, I'm Cayla Marlow-Beaumont."

Helen Marlow rolled her eyes and sucked her teeth with the same sound he'd heard Kimber produce whenever irritated. "She's Cay Beaumont. I don't understand why you young women have to hyphenate your names."

Tight-lipped, Cay Marlow-Beaumont patted her grandmother's shoulder. "Because we want to preserve the prestigious Marlow name."

"Whatever."

Nate hid his smile.

"Boy, you better hurry up and get over to the table," Grandmamma Helen barked, "instead of standing over here drooling like a fool. Parker will done scoop Amelia right out from under you."

"Grandmamma…" Cay said, frowning with disapproval. "I'm sorry, she's ready for her nap."

Out the corner of his eye, he saw Cay wheel her grandmother away under loud protest. The commotion she caused captured everyone's attention. Parker Ward, the fireman, turned and nodded his head in Nate's direction. Nate scratched his beard, not sure what to do. Did he interrupt them? Now this was complicated. Clearly they had been an item once before. Was it puppy love or her first real love? Nate didn't want to find out. Instead of turning around like his brain told him to, he stalked across the room toward the table. Parker stood and extended his hand, probably to show he was being the bigger guy.

"I came to collect you," Nate said to Amelia after showing he was the bigger man by shaking Parker's hand.

"Where has the afternoon gone?" Amelia clutched the

pearls at her throat again and stood up. "Parker, I enjoyed catching up with you."

"Maybe you'll save me a dance at Emily's wedding," Parker went on. "She told me she ran into you last night."

And wasn't it Emily who wanted to keep her visit to the pizzeria a secret? Nate smirked as a thunderous cloud darkened the window. "Hey, we better get going if we're going to beat the rain before it gets to the house."

Amelia offered a wave goodbye before following Nate outside. He didn't slow his pace so she could walk beside him. Instead of walking to the beat of his heart, he stormed out to the beat of his pounding anger. Amelia's flat shoes walked quickly behind him.

"What the hell is your problem?" she screamed over another clap of thunder.

"I don't have one." Nate maneuvered his way through the parking lot, hating himself. "Let's go."

"I think I'll walk." The patter of Amelia's flat shoes ceased. He turned to face her, finding her standing on the curb with her hand on her hip. Fat drops of water hit the ground, sizzling away with the heat.

Nate smirked. "Walk, or go inside and catch a ride with Parker. Maybe that's what you want."

"I don't understand what's going on with you, Nate," Amelia said. Rain began to fall harder. Nate stalked back toward her, damned if he let Parker save the day—again.

"I don't share."

"We're not children and this isn't kindergarten." Amelia squared her shoulders. Water pegged the two of them. His chest rose with desire as the material soaked her dress.

"I don't share," he said again.

She opened to protest but he captured her by the back of her neck with one hand and dragged his face down to hers for a deep, soul-silencing kiss.

Chapter 7

The front seat of his SUV crackled with sexual tension. Like this morning, they drove in utter silence. Unlike this morning, Nate understood where this was going. The kiss he shared with Amelia generated its own lightning. He drove like a madman down County Road Seventeen to get back to the house. He thought nothing was going to stop them, but up ahead the red lights of the train tracks began to flash. Not wanting to chance the timing of the train, Nate veered to the right and pulled off to the side of the road into a cut of the woods in case other cars pulled up to the flashing lights. Heavy raindrops pounded the rooftop, filling the inside of the vehicle with a deafening noise when he cut off the engine. The darkness of the trees, thanks to the dreary clouds, helped conceal their position if anyone drove by.

Amelia turned in her seat to face him. The window behind her fogged with her body heat. Her red, completely kissable lips opened with question. Nate leaned across the console between them and pressed his lips against hers as if to answer. Her sweet breath touched the corners of his mouth. Aroused beyond desire, he pressed further into the kiss. The damn console prevented him from truly getting to her like he wanted, but he settled for a trail of kisses along her neck.

Amelia cupped his neck; her thumb traced his bulging vein, throbbing with desire. The material of her dress, now soaked, clung to her skin. A damn good way to find out she wasn't wearing a bra. Nate smiled and dipped his head lower, tracing a finger along the swell of the top of her breast. Her chest expanded, urging him to probe further. The side of his forefinger brushed against a bud and twirling it between his two fingers he manipulated it into a hard nub.

Soft fingers caressed against the nape of his neck. Nate dipped his head a little lower and captured her other nipple in his mouth. A mew escaped Amelia's throat. Hips thrusting forward, Nate took his cue and reached between her thighs. She propped one wet foot on the seat and opened her legs wider for him. A wave of desire washed over him as his fingers pushed aside her panties and sunk into the wet flesh. The shoulders of the white dress stretched and he pulled them down, exposing her deep pink nipples to him. His mouth watered. His other hand reached behind and to the side to lower her seat. From his new angle, he was able to have better access to her other breast and still toy with the wet folds. His fingers delved farther and the palm of his hand ground against her. She grounded her hips back. Harder. Longer. Amelia's hands grasped for the headrest.

Why she'd decided to hold out on him for the last few nights was beyond him, but this pent-up desire only proved his point. *She wanted him.* The strain against his jeans indicated how much he wanted her right now, but he was too busy watching the rise and fall of her chest from breathing so hard with each deeper stroke he made into her with his hand. They moved in unison just as he remembered at the hotel. Faster. Nate leaned back in his seat, watching Amelia's face as she came in his hands. The corners of her eyes crinkled. Her mouth made the cutest O shape and when she clenched against his fingers, her face softened angelically.

"Oh, my God," she breathed. The raindrops slowed as her breathing regulated. Lazily she rolled her head to the left and opened one eye. "Why are you staring at me?"

"Because you're beautiful."

Amelia covered her face with her hands at the reality of what they'd just done. "Oh, God, this is crazy."

"Crazy is denying us this," Nate said, taking her hand away from her face. He caressed her soft cheek.

"I didn't buy you for this."

Nate's laugh reverberated off the interior of the car. "Thanks for making me feel sleazy."

After a quick tug of her hand from his, Amelia playfully swatted his chest. "Shut up. That's not what I meant."

"I know." Nate recaptured her hand and kissed her fingertips. "You want forty hours of work from me and you'll get it."

"It doesn't matter anymore, Nate." She sighed.

"Why not?"

"Because we've crossed a line between us, and now what will everyone think?"

"What line? Between employee and employer?" he guessed. "This is ridiculous. What do we care whatever anyone else thinks? Who's going to know?"

"What about the last time something like this happened between us?"

"Do you regret it?" he asked of her.

For a heartbeat she waited to answer. A strange vise tightened around Nate's heart until she spoke. "Look where I ended up."

"You mean, back in your hometown with me as your most prized possession?" Nate teased and tugged on her hand in preparation of her trying to pull away. "How 'bout I finish the work at your grandmother's house and then we can talk about us?"

"What *us*, Nate?" She pulled her hand away again and succeeded.

"Why not an *us*?" he asked, not sure if he truly heard the words coming out of his mouth. "It's not like you have a job to rush back to. Stay here in Southwood and at least see where we can go."

Amelia stifled a laugh, covering the mouth he'd kissed, and glanced out the window. "Go where?"

"Emily's wedding, for starters."

"Even if I wanted to," Amelia groaned, "I didn't bring any sort of wedding attire."

Glad she was beginning to warm up to his idea, Nate smiled. "Well, I have the perfect person for you to meet. You may already know her, she's from here."

Amelia turned fully toward him. "Who?"

With the way her voice went up in question, Nate wanted to learn more about what made Amelia so distrustful toward the residents of Southwood. She told him the people had turned on her and her family, but he'd never understood how. So far everyone they ran into acted like they missed Amelia. Everyone had accepted him and Stephen—well, at least him—so easily. "My future sister-in-law, Lexi Pendergrass."

"I didn't know her personally. She went to a different school," said Amelia, the corners of her mouth turning downward. "My parents knew hers. Of course everyone knows her parents."

He didn't miss the way Amelia rolled her eyes. Then again, Lexi did the same thing whenever someone brought up her parents. "I wonder what time it is. We can probably go back and see her at her shop."

"What shop?"

"Grits and Glam Gowns," Nate said proudly. "She has all kinds of froufrou dresses you might like."

Amelia frowned. "I don't do froufrou and it's about four-thirty."

Nate sat up and turned the engine on. The blue lights indicated the time and Amelia's correctness. He glanced over and caught her smug smile. "Hey," she said, sitting up and readjusting her top, "that's how it is in the summer. Always carry an umbrella."

"I'm a man, Amelia." He gave a sideways grin and began backing out of the cut. "I always carry protection."

Monday afternoon's shower halted any of the outside work Nate planned on doing that evening. But he continued clocking in his hours by helping her move the heavy things downstairs to her grandmamma's new room. By the time they completed their project, they were too tired to move.

Tuesday morning, Amelia woke up on one section of the L-shaped couch in the TV room, lying against Nate's broad chest while he stretched out on the other half. His soft snoring soothed her. A heavy arm draped protectively around her and his fingers spanned against her hips. Black stubble was sprinkled across his chiseled cheeks.

Between the opening of the kitchen and the stairs, the

grandfather clock ticked away. If she were working, she would have been up before the crack of dawn, prepping her camera crew about what she wanted filmed. Sleeping in was not a luxury she could afford. She wondered what Natalia was up to or if she was getting along with William. Rory hadn't called to give her an update and the restriction on contact worked both ways. No one was to call her. She hadn't even heard her phone ring once.

Thinking of her phone, Amelia reached for hers off the square glass coffee table. She pressed the buttons for the screen saver to come to life. The half beat of the light flipped on, then turned off. She caught a quick glimpse of the problem. She needed to charge her phone; if only she remembered where she placed her bag with her charger.

Amelia peeled herself away from Nate's grip with a bit of ease. As she rolled over onto the white carpet, she went on her hands and knees, careful not to wake him. Thankfully the black leggings and the off-shoulder red Alabama shirt in which she'd fallen asleep absorbed the irritating material of Grandmamma's carpet. Nate shifted with a snort and his right hand sought the comfort of her body. Amelia reached up and grabbed one of the fluffy throw pillows braced against the back of the couch and slipped it under his hand. A pout tugged at the corners of her lips when the plump material seemed to satisfy Nate. His steady snore continued.

Jealous of a pillow? Disgusted with herself, Amelia headed off down the hall beyond the steps, toward the area now designated for the new study. They'd set up the room with a desktop computer; on the beige wall, Nate had hung one of the flat-screen televisions they'd found elsewhere in the house. A small leather couch folded out in one corner. Maybe this Christmas everyone would gather here for the holidays. Amelia stopped in her tracks. Since when did she think about coming here—period?

Just because Emily was courteous to her did not mean she was welcome back into the fold of Southwood society. Not like she wanted to be welcomed back. Amelia opened some of the drawers in hopes of finding a charger. She then headed into her grandmamma's new room looking for a charger. She didn't want to run up the stairs unless she had to. Since her episode in the car with Nate, Amelia doubted her legs would take the unnecessary stretching of the steps.

Hopefully Grandmamma wouldn't yell at her for searching her drawers. Nate had suggested they move the drawers down individually but clearly he did not understand how picky Grandmamma was. So completing the backbreaking task worked out better than being killed by Grandmamma for allowing a man to see her personals. Before she even delved into the big dresser drawers, Amelia sat on the edge of Grandmamma's queen-size bed. When she and her parents had come to live here, Amelia remembered sitting there getting life lessons. Of course, now Amelia realized Grandmamma's life lessons were more warnings about how to treat others and how she expected to be treated. Nothing stuck.

Sighing, Amelia reached for the drawer of the nightstand. Expectedly, she found a Bible. This was the same Bible her grandmother carried to church every Sunday. The cover was worn, the pages frail and filled with yellow highlighter marks. A faint trace of Chanel No. 5 rose from it. Amelia smiled and reached around in the drawer for anything feeling remotely like a cord. Some form of plastic scratched her fingertips. Amelia pulled her hand back to investigate the culprit. What she found caused her to jump off the bed. Condoms! She glanced down briefly and remembered this dresser used to be in her bedroom upstairs. Were these her condoms from years ago?

"Kill me," Amelia groaned, shoving them to the back of the drawer.

"Everything okay?"

Amelia spun around and died a few more deaths at the sight of Nate's bare chest again, leaning against the doorjamb. How did one really say what she found? That she was having sex in high school in her grandmother's house? If her father didn't exist, Amelia would have been positive her grandmamma had never had sex in here. Now either she didn't know what the condoms were for or she left them in the drawer to one day fall down the steps, knowing Amelia would be the one to come here and move things around. Sure, the latter seemed more outrageous, but Amelia worked in reality TV; she knew crazy.

"Oh, nothing," Amelia said sweetly, plastering a smile across her face. Her eyes traveled to the V stemming from the muscles of his stomach.

"Were you looking for something?"

In attempt to nod her head and shake it at the same time, Amelia ended up rotating her head in a circular motion. "Um, yes, but never mind. Good morning, did I wake you?"

"Yes, when you left my side." Nate crossed his arms. The tribal tattoo seemed to ripple across his arm and chest. "Did my snoring wake you?"

"No, I'm used to waking up this early."

Nate's eyes widened. "This is early for you?"

"Yes."

"It's almost eleven," he smirked.

Amelia widened her eyes the same way he had. "You're kidding me."

He reached into the front of his jeans for his cell phone

and swiped the screen. Besides the time, the first thing she noticed was the photograph of two adorable girls in a selfie pose with Nate. "Your nieces?"

"Kimber and Philly," Nate said proudly. "They're in school now, or should be, provided my brother got up in time." She must have squinted her eyes because Nate nodded his head and took her by the hand. "Trust me, it's happened in the past. Let's get some coffee in us and then we'll head over to Grits and Glam Gowns."

Amelia sat at the kitchen table and watched Nate make his way around the room. She toyed with the vase holding the long-stemmed daisies he'd brought her yesterday. Will she ever be able to look at daisies again without thinking of him? Inhaling deeply, Amelia focused on Nate's backside. He was comfortable in here. He might as well be; he'd nearly set it on fire and then cleaned every spot like a professional. There was no trace of smoke at all. Grandmamma would never know what happened, let alone that someone else tried cooking in her kitchen. God, how the old woman complained whenever Amelia's mother tried to help out and prepare a meal, Amelia thought bitterly. When the coffee finished percolating, Nate poured them each a mug and joined her at the table.

"So when you're not sleeping in until eleven," Nate asked, "what time do you normally get up?"

"It depends." Amelia shrugged her shoulders. "If I'm working as a field producer, the perfume ad for the Ruizes kept me pretty busy since we were filming out on location. The ads for the perfume were going to be shown on an upcoming episode. I'd have to film every moment of their lives, including getting into their rooms before they woke up."

"Sounds boring."

"To most," said Amelia, "it might. But I campaigned

to be on their show. Their storyline is incredible and not one typical in the realm of reality shows."

"Because they're not simply beautiful people, but also business folks, as well?" he asked and immediately explained. "Turns out the sixteen-year-old watches your show and she loves them."

"Well, you have to love the Ruizes," said Amelia.

Nate propped his elbows on the table. "No, I don't. I know them, remember?"

"Oh, yes," Amelia said, grinning sheepishly. "You were going to tell me why your brother and Natalia were meeting that night."

"Nice try." He shook his head.

Amelia rolled her eyes. "Damn."

"Maybe she'll be in town for the Crystal Coquí Ball," he said, smiling over the rim of his coffee. "By the way, my mother is looking forward to meeting you. She already worships the ground you walk on."

Heart speeding up, Amelia shook her head back and forth. "What?"

"My ma believes everyone needs to be introduced to the Puerto Rican life, and you're a pioneer in her eyes, thanks to your show, *Azúcar*. So, Labor Day weekend you're coming with me."

The way he stated she'd come with him somehow excited Amelia. A flash of desire quivered in the pit of her belly. The last thing she wanted was to allow him to think his machismo turned her on, so she rolled her eyes and took another sip of her coffee. She was surprised how naturally the rest of their conversation grew. She learned more about his family and the girls. Kimber was a handful and Philly had him wrapped around his finger. Nate didn't elaborate on why he had not attended college after his high school graduation and she for once didn't press the issue. Amelia wondered if she would have wanted to go off to another school right after enduring a campus shooting. The story editor in her wanted to create a reunion of everyone affected by the school shooting. Had any of the survivors sought the arms of a fellow survivor, and had the relationship lasted? Did anyone stay in town after the shooting? Judging from the twitch in Nate's jaw whenever she alluded to the event, she figured it best to leave her ideas alone.

After they shared a few stories and two cups of coffee, Amelia headed upstairs to shower, offering Nate the bathroom downstairs. Ready to spend more time with Nate, Amelia dressed in a pair of ivory lace shorts and a matching short-sleeve top, and since she was heading to a glam shop, she put on some heels. Nate greeted her with a whistle and met her at the bottom of the steps with a kiss. He'd changed out of his jeans into a pair of khaki cargo shorts and a button-down preppy green Oxford opened at the throat. For a man, his feet, encased in a pair of tan canvas flip-flops, looked pretty damn good.

In the span of forty-eight hours since Nate had arrived on the property after following her, they'd gone from awkward silence to a passionate episode in his car to now holding hands as he drove down the back streets toward town. Dread no longer flashed in the pit of her stomach as the folks walking down the street waved. She didn't think about what anyone had to say to her about her past. The only thing that concerned her was what Nate's beloved family would think of her.

Any indication they might hold some form of resentment against her was washed away the moment the bells over the door of Lexi's shop chimed and everyone cooed all over her. For starters, Lexi was a dream. Amelia slightly remembered seeing photos of her in the gossip headlines about a scandalous beauty queen. Whatever Lexi's past, Amelia had no room to judge, especially when the tall blonde towered over her and wrapped her arms around her shoulders.

"I am so happy to finally meet you," Lexi Pendergrass said dramatically. "It's about time someone else starts a ruckus around here besides me."

At the beauty queen's emphasis on *finally*, Amelia glanced nervously over Lexi's shoulder toward Nate. As Lexi pulled back and straightened, she shook her head. "Didn't Nate tell you about all the trouble I've stirred up around here?"

"I don't get into the gossip." Nate rolled his eyes toward Amelia.

"I've had my own brush with Southwood scandals," Amelia said.

A tall, beefy man literally waltzed over to them. "Southwood Scandals," he said. "I like it. Andrew Mason, at your service."

"Nice to meet you, Andrew." Amelia took the man's meaty hand. "I'm Amelia Marlow."

"Oh, girl, I know all about you," Andrew gushed. "I've followed your career since your show, *The Real Divas of College Park*."

A warmth of embarrassment rose from Amelia's chest to her cheeks. "Not one of my finest."

"What's this?" Nate leaned back to get a better look at her.

"One of the first shows I produced."

"With the cattiest women in the world," Andrew interjected. "But the best times were when you had to step on camera and yank those women apart. Talk about a weave war."

Lexi cocked her head to the side and grinned. "You're

embarrassing her, Andrew. Go away." She took Amelia by the arm and led her through the rows and racks of dresses—not ones Amelia thought were appropriate for a wedding. "Don't fear. I'm in the middle of remodeling."

A good storefront makeover was what Lexi apparently needed. For starters, she had too many dresses in one area, separated by colors. Amelia practically walked through a rainbow before Lexi brought her to the back of the store to a set of steps.

"I've got some dresses up here."

Amelia followed Lexi up a set of wrought-iron stairs winding their way up to an open-floored loft. All types and sizes of mannequins filled the room with different styles of dresses. Short dresses made for children, long, prom-style dresses and wedding gowns hung in clear plastic wrap from satin hangers.

"Did you sew all of these?" Amelia asked in awe.

"I did." Lexi nodded and surprised Amelia by blushing. "I wish my niece didn't leave for school early. We call her the Dress Whisperer. Oh, I have a great idea. Stand over there." Lexi spoke a mile a minute and pointed toward the red couch shaped like a pair of lips.

Reluctantly Amelia stood by the couch. A gold-laminated oval mirror hung over the brick wall behind the couch. Lexi stood in front of her and used her phone to take a photo of Amelia. The flash blinded her momentarily.

"Sorry, but I'm going to send this to Jolene."

"Your niece?"

Nodding, Lexi waved her hand to the couch and gracefully folded herself into a director's chair. "Tell me about yourself, Amelia. Nate mentioned over the phone about you being from here but not wanting to come back."

"Well," Amelia started, not wanting to offend. Lexi hadn't grown up in Southwood like she did. Lexi's parents were well-off and sent her away to boarding school out of state; she came home to Southwood with her friends for the summer. She'd come back and made something of herself. "I'm not fond of being back here."

"Bad memories?"

"Let's say I don't expect to be inducted in the town's hall of fame any time soon."

"Girl, you either?" Lexi slapped her long leg. "And my folks are on the committee."

Amelia decided she liked Lexi and her spunk. "So are you in the pageant business or the wedding business?" She waved her hand toward the mannequin with the long white train.

"Both. Right now the pageant world is hot but it's about to die down since school's started. I've always loved to sew, and original pageant dresses are the way to go for a one-of-a-kind."

"O-O-A-K." Amelia grinned.

"You know your pageant terminology."

Amelia shook her head and confessed, "I know my reality show competition. Why haven't you been on one of the shows?"

"No way. Those shows take away the good and put an evil spin on something innocent." Lexi's hand covered her mouth. "I'm so sorry," she mumbled.

"No offense taken," Amelia said with a laugh. "A lot of shows do prey on people. I can't say I've never gotten my hands dirty when I started but I'd like to think I've grown."

"With Natalia Ruiz's show?"

Aware now of the history between Natalia and Nate's brother, Amelia pressed her lips together. Of course Lexi saw the story on the Real-A-Tea blog—as well as Amelia's oversight. The irresponsible anonymous blogger was a bane in everyone's existence. The person behind the computer screen had a mole at every reality show.

Before growing angry again, Amelia swallowed her feelings. "Yes."

"She's a beautiful woman."

"She is," Amelia agreed. Amelia studied the beauty queen's face for a moment and tried to gauge a read. Nate was still tight-lipped about the reason Natalia had met with Stephen. Did Lexi know? "You're not worried about her and Stephen?"

"Nah." Lexi waved off the notion without a wrinkle in her face. "What I am worried about is the Keaton wedding."

Ah, a girl concerned with business first. Amelia liked her even more. "Are you afraid something is going to happen?"

"Well, I've had a lot of rave reviews and new customers brought in because of the pageant business, but the last wedding dress I believe jinxed me."

The ivory dress on the mannequin with its sweetheart neckline and full skirt was beautiful. Every intricate stitch was perfect. "I swear I won't attend the wedding." She held two fingers together in the air.

"Not *you*," said Lexi, reaching out and playfully waving off the notion with a flick of her wrist. "You better come. We're about to pick out the best dress, if Jolene will ever text back. I'm talking about the last dress I made. The bride disappeared."

Amelia pressed her lips together and watched through half-closed eyes as Lexi fretted. "What do you mean disappeared?"

"I mean, slipped out the back door and no one has heard from her."

"Where was this wedding?" Amelia sat up straight. "Was this in Orlando?"

"Yes, how did you know?"

"When I'm not working, I live there in an apartment. Well, used to." Amelia shook her head to get to the point. "Are you talking about the Ramos-Montenegro wedding?"

"You know Grace?" Lexi's mouth gaped open.

"I know the groom, well, the-would-have-been-groom, Ricardo." Amelia sank into the cushions of the red couch and briefly explained her job at MET and how they were going to document the life of the young congressman, and the footage filmed leading up to the wedding and the ceremony itself would be aired on their network. Amelia had offered to edit the footage, but with the bride disappearing, her project had ended. She'd pitched an idea to Rory about trying to find the bride, a local chef, but Rory thought it was too soon.

"So you edit film?"

"I used to. I have a team who pores over the twenty-four hours of footage and then comes up with a storyboard for a forty-four minute show."

Lexi perked up. "But you have experience."

"Sure. Do you need help with something?"

"Well," Lexi said, nodding eagerly, "my assistant, Chantal, has been following Emily and her fiancé around all week, leading up to the wedding. I'm determined to put something nice together for them but I'm afraid I'm going to overdo it on the footage or ramble. I don't want the video to be boring."

Flattered, Amelia nodded. "I'd be honored to don my story producer crown to help."

"You're already familiar with the terminology." The beauty queen beamed.

"Let's get some tea while we wait for Jolene." Lexi

stood and rubbed her hands against her pink slacks. "I don't have to explain there's sugar in it, do I?"

"Hell no."

"Ugh," Lexi moaned playfully and held her hand out to help Amelia to her feet. "Those Reyes men, gotta love 'em, eh?"

Love? Hmm, nah. Amelia shook off the notion and allowed Lexi to lead her into the kitchen. Love didn't happen in the span of forty-eight hours. She'd tried putting two weeks of footage once into a believable fairy tale of falling in love in two days—completely unbelievable.

Chapter 8

"You're smiling," said Stephen Reyes, leaning against his brother's shoulders to state the obvious.

Nate's eyes swept over the toothy grin across Amelia's face, laughing at whatever one of her friends just whispered in her ear. Shrugging his brother's hand off, Nate rose from his spot on the couch, careful not to knock over the low round table filled with drinks of various sizes in Southern Charm's VIP section.

Amelia Marlow sauntered toward him the only way Amelia could—seductively. He'd spotted her the moment she walked into the club, flanked by Lexi and Amelia's cousin and looking more suited for a music video than a combined bachelor and bachelorette party. With the exception of the groom, every single man in the club had damn near broken his neck—in Nate's eyes—for a peek at Amelia and her gorgeous long legs. Her height didn't measure up to her cousin's or Lexi's, but she held her head high as a princess. The sway of her hips had his head moving from side to side. A strange brew of jealousy and desire twisted in his gut. He didn't play the jealous type; however, his body craved another taste of Amelia. When he recognized the combination, Nate started to regret agreeing to come, but now he was pleasantly surprised.

"Nice to see you out," Amelia's strawberry-tinted lips mouthed. "Enjoying yourself?"

The contemporary song bounced off the speakers in all four corners of the VIP room. The volume made hearing her next to impossible, which Nate appreciated. Amelia stopped a half an inch from him, bringing along with her a sweet berry scent. His mouth watered but not for the fruit.

"I am now," he answered. Instinctively his arms went around her shoulders. She pressed her light-colored fingernails against the fabric of his black T-shirt. The soft touch evoked an automatic erection, which strained against the fabric of his tan chinos. Nate cleared his throat. "I am surprised you came tonight."

"I hadn't planned on coming out," Amelia said with a grim smile, "but since you kicked me out of the house I didn't have many choices."

"I didn't kick you out," said Nate, making air quotes with his fingers. "I just needed to concentrate on finishing up the work."

"Thanks for kicking her out." Lexi danced her way over to the two of them, wrapping her arms around their shoulders. "I needed to get out of my apartment, too."

Cay came over, slapped her arms around Amelia and Nate's shoulders, as well. "Whew, I needed to get out of the house. Those kids were driving me nuts."

"Don't talk about my babies." Amelia winked at Nate. The corners of his mouth twisted with relief as she flirted with him. "She forgets she left the house last week."

"Don't forget—" Cay rolled her eyes "—you left me to find my own way home."

A sweet, champagne-scented breath blew across his face when Amelia sighed in sarcasm. "I did you a favor. I called Gregory to come and get you. Don't try and tell me the two of you did not take advantage of an evening alone."

Gregory, the man Nate was introduced to earlier by Stephen, walked over to the group and asked his wife to dance. Stephen took the cue and led Lexi off. Alone, Nate wrapped his arms around Amelia's waist. "I like what you're wearing."

"It's a romper." Amelia stepped out of his arms to twirl her frame. "Lexi insisted I get it."

"She does know her fashion." Nate made a mental note to thank his future sister-in-law.

"Yes." Amelia stepped back into his arms. "But does she know how to take this off?"

Nate raised a brow. "Already trying to get naked for me?"

As a licensed contractor and real estate agent, Nate did not like the idea of milking the time on one project. The forty hours Amelia had paid for had gone by quicker than expected, especially since the episode Monday in the front seat of his SUV. Nate had decided he'd refrain from taking advantage of Amelia until he finished the job. He had diligently worked his forty hours, finishing up this morning when he turned off the engine of the cement truck at five. Now when Helen Marlow came home Monday morning, she'd get inside with the ramp hidden behind her bushes right up to her porch.

Had it not been for the rain, the job may have been done earlier. A part of Nate was thankful for the bad weather. It had given him a chance to help Amelia with some heavy lifting and get to know her better. Besides rearranging the furniture, they'd sorted through the items in the breezeway. Amelia reminisced over each piece of equipment from her family's business. It suffered the most when the locals stopped coming in for ice cream. Eventually, her parents had to shut the shop down. His heart ached at the sound of the pain in her voice.

Trying to maintain his gentlemanly reputation over the last three days with Amelia had been hard. *Literally*. Tuesday evening, Amelia had bent fully over into the deep freezer, trying to find a container of homemade ice cream. Her lace shorts roamed his dreams that night—at least the pieces he imaginarily shredded off her frame did. Wednesday morning, she had stepped out onto the porch in the smallest pair of denim shorts ever and a bright yellow halter top. She'd had the nerve to break out an old-fashioned ice-cream maker and wrap her legs around the brown wooden bucket as she turned the crank; Nate should have been inducted into sainthood. Hearing the shower every morning drove him insane with the temptation to peep through the barn's window. At least he sought a bit of mental revenge by bringing Amelia daisies every day. She might not have had any idea why he chose the flowers and in a sick twisted way it satisfied him even more.

"No one is trying to get naked for you. You're crazy." Amelia laughed, pressing her hand against his beating heart, bringing him out of his trance. Did she feel the way his heart beat for her? Nate glanced down to where her hands curled against his chest.

Nate cleared his throat and willed his body to stay in control with the mental image of Amelia stepping out of this romper in front of him while he sat in a chair. The only thing he focused on was the spot on her glass where her lips curled. Nate took her by the hand and led her back to the low table where he and a few of the guys were sitting. A waitress came by and took away the empty glasses and wiped up the wet circles where the glasses had sweat.

"Are you having fun tonight?" Amelia turned toward him in the couch. She pulled her right leg up onto the couch to angle herself better to see him. Nate's eyes grazed over the triangle she made with her legs. The hem of the shorts rolled up, offering a view of the sweet nectar his hands wanted to have the pleasure of seeking.

"Me?" Nate realized he'd leaned too close to her. He sat straight up and looked forward, counting to ten backward and in Spanish. "I'm enjoying myself now." Body settled, he turned toward her and bumped her shoulders with his.

The waitress returned with two more glasses of champagne. "Sam didn't hold back on the expenses tonight," he said.

"I'm sure he's grateful Emily stuck by him all these years," Amelia said, draining the drink in hand before taking another. "Did I tell you the two of them were the first to break the ice for all of us in the same class? She invited him to our Sadie Hawkins dance and they were the first boy-girl pair to dance together. Can you imagine?"

"Uh, no." Nate tried to contain his laughter.

"I bet you were asked by all the girls in your graduating class." Amelia brushed a piece of lint off his left shoulder and let her hand lie there. Her fingertips drew circles on his collarbone.

"Not all." He shrugged off the memory. "Remember, half the girls were related to me."

"Ah, the infamous Torres clan."

Nate nodded his head. "You don't believe me?"

"No."

"Dating in Villa San Juan was hard," said Nate. "I had to check all the girls' family trees before asking them out."

"Aw, you poor thing," she cooed against his ear. "Is

that why you left town? Did you go through all the women there?"

"If I hadn't…" Nate cocked his head to the side and leaned closer. His lips brushed against hers. "I wouldn't be here with you."

"Well, let's toast to getting off the island." Amelia left his side for a moment to grab new glasses of champagne for the two of them. Nate gave her wrist a gentle push for her to set the drinks back down. Instead of taking what she offered, he took a kiss. His hands sunk into her silky hair and brought her face closer.

Everything else around them blurred out of his mind. Nate closed his eyes, wishing they were anywhere but here. Amelia's sweet lips opened for him and it took no coaxing of his mouth to taste her tongue. Three days of no touching or kissing came out with the kiss. Nate pulled Amelia into his lap. She straddled his legs and cupped his face with her soft hands, eager for more. He loved the way her hands roamed through his hair. His leg threatened to twitch when her fingernails scratched his scalp. If ever he wondered about heaven, he got a taste of it sliding his hands down her waist and grabbing a handful of her butt cheeks. The tempo of the music set the pace of each stroke she ground down on his hard body. Amelia broke the kiss only to torture him more, nibbling his ear once, then turning his head to face the other direction of the VIP room so she could give him some more of her sweet torture.

In the heartbeat of a changeover between songs, someone above them cleared his throat. Nate wanted to curse his brother out but reality hit him. Any moment now, the rest of the wedding party would find them up here in this position. Gently Nate pulled Amelia against him in a bear hug. "We have company," he whispered into her ear.

"Whoops." Amelia smoothly slid off his lap and stood

up, using the sides of her thumb and index finger to wipe away any remnants of her makeup. Too late; he'd already kissed it off. While Amelia inconspicuously tugged at the hem of her romper, Nate lounged back in the cushions. The crew she'd walked in with made their way up the steps but turned to follow Amelia. "I think I may need to freshen up my lipstick."

Stephen watched the three women walk off, waiting until they disappeared down the steps. "Bruh, what are you doing?"

"I thought I was spending time with Amelia. What's up?"

"Brittany is here."

Nate shrugged his shoulders. "So?"

"So?" Stephen mocked his brother. "She's been pissed off since she hasn't seen you all week."

Nate shrugged. "Again, so? I am not with Brittany and I've made myself perfectly clear."

Stephen sighed and scratched the top of his bald head. "She thinks you're taking her to the wedding."

Nate did not understand why the teacher would think so. He'd made himself clear he did not bring women to weddings—at least not usually. Amelia was different. She didn't ask him questions about where their relationship was headed.

Wait, why didn't she? Nate sat up straight. Sure she'd only been in town for a week now, but she was getting used to the idea, right? What if she left? Where would she go? Did they need to have the talk about where this relationship was heading? *No*, he refused to have it. *And why not?* A voice nagged at him. Because once they had the talk, things became complicated. Things always became complicated when he had "the talk" with women he dated. His biggest focus now was his nieces. The women he'd met so far were quick to want to start a family with him and play mother to Philly and Kimber. Before moving to Southwood, women tried to acknowledge him on their social media pages as their boyfriend or significant other, thus bringing in more drama for him from the others he dated.

He did not do complicated.

Despite the ridiculously high heels Lexi and Cay had talked her into wearing, Amelia coasted into the women's bathroom on cloud nine. The moment the doors closed, the music ceased and after that episode in the VIP room, Amelia's heartbeat echoed even louder in her ears.

"So what music were the two of you listening to up there?" Cay teased, adjusting the level of her voice.

"We practically had to use a machete to cut through all the sexual tension between you and Nate," added Lexi.

Amelia missed moments like this—not like she experienced them herself. In her years as a young producer, she'd captured the moments of camaraderie of young ladies gushing over guys. Amelia never expected to be the subject of such a topic. "Hush," she told them.

"Check out the grin." Cay elbowed Lexi, her new bestie. It comforted Amelia knowing Cay had gained a new friend. Lexi had already talked Cay into bringing her kids to a pageant. At least when Amelia went back to work Cay had someone to turn to. "I haven't seen her grin since she packed up her bags and left town."

Ignoring the two of them, Amelia reached in her pocket for her favorite strawberry lip gloss. Despite the makeover Lexi and Cay had talked her into today, she still recognized herself a bit. She hardly ever got the chance to wear her hair loose and free. Lexi must have amped up Amelia's shoulder-length hair with sex appeal. Men never turned to take a second look at her, and yet tonight she'd been swarmed by single guys asking her to dance. For once, she felt glamorous and wondered if this was what Natalia went through on a daily basis.

Perhaps her newfound confidence had brought on her sexual energy upstairs with Nate. Nate being as hot as he was helped fuel the flames. Who knew not seeing him for a full day would spark such desire? Maybe she did need to get laid again. Didn't Natalia always tell her such crude stuff?

"You saw me grinning in the rearview mirror when I left town." Amelia side-eyed her cousin in the refection in the mirror. Using her pinky finger, she swiped the extra bit of gloss off the bottom center of her lip and the divot of her cupid's bow. "And as soon as Grandmamma is well, I'll show you the same grin again."

"Amelia," Cay scolded.

Lexi stood in front of the mirror and pretended to fuss with her blond hair. "You're not leaving any time soon, are you?"

"She was ordered a mandatory month off to take care of our grandmother," Cay explained. "She's been here a week."

"Good." Lexi beamed. "That gives us three more weeks to convince her to stay."

In the reflection Amelia also watched the center stall door open. Irritation replaced her bliss. Amelia rolled her eyes and sighed heavily. So far tonight she was having a good time.

"Amelia." Brittany Foley gave her reflection a curt, chilly nod.

"Brittany." Amelia returned the icy stare.

Lexi cut the tension by clearing her throat, as if with an imaginary machete. "Brittany, what a surprise to run into you tonight."

"Really, Lexi?" Brittany snapped. "I told you on the first day of school I'd be attending all of Emily's events. She was my best friend, after all. I'm the one who's been by her side after everything. I recall telling you today at the bridal shower hosted by Emily's mother I'd see you tonight."

The jab was meant to cut Amelia but at the moment she didn't care. She turned and faced her alleged opponent. "Let's cut to the chase, Brittany."

"Let's." Brittany folded her arms across her flat chest. The flowery dress she wore with a pair of white sandals did nothing for her figure. The church mouse act didn't fool Amelia one bit.

Some of the women already in line for the bathroom turned around to leave. The last thing Amelia wanted to do was to cause a scene at Emily's event. In the years of following women around, especially after they'd been drinking, Amelia had witnessed a loss of common sense in women and a false sense of bravado.

"You're upset because I'm back in town and you fear there's something going on between me and Nate?"

Taken aback by Amelia's bluntness, Brittany stuttered to find her words. "Nate and I are working on things."

A week ago, Amelia may have believed such a thing but not anymore. "I'm sorry to interrupt your plans, Brittany, I really am. But I am not in town for some competition."

"Why exactly are you back?"

"Brittany," Cay interjected. "Let's not hash out things here in the women's bathroom. Not tonight."

"Contrary to your own popular belief, Brittany," said Amelia sarcastically, "I don't owe you an explanation as to why I'm here. And while I'm here, I will do whatever I want with whomever I want. Do I make myself clear?"

"Exactly," Brittany said with a smirk. "Because you just told me you don't plan on being here long."

"What?"

"Don't worry about it, Amelia." Brittany pronounced every syllable in Amelia's name. "I'm on to you. And if you break Nate's heart before you leave, we're going to have another conversation."

If the woman hadn't been so pathetic, Amelia would have laughed in her face. Who would have guessed the pastor's granddaughter to have such a possessive streak? "You're cute, Brittany. And I will let you in on a little secret. I don't plan on being here long but in the meantime, you need to make sure you stay out of my path."

Brittany waved her hand toward the door. "Well, please go first. I already know what it's like to be in the path of your destruction. Clearly everyone else around town has forgotten."

Amelia shook her head and rolled her eyes toward the ceiling. "Despite what you may think, Brittany, I'm not the threat here."

"I'll believe that when you…uh, what was it you said a few moments ago?" Brittany smirked. "Have the city behind you in your rearview mirror."

Amelia took a deep breath in exasperation. "I give up. Ladies," she said to Lexi and Cay, "I'll see you upstairs."

Music deafened Amelia's ears the moment she opened the door. Lights from the spinning disco ball blinded her for a moment. She blinked but each time she tried to adjust her sight, the lights flashed dark. A large, warm hand wrapped around her wrist and dragged her onto the dance floor. For a split second she thought Nate had come to rescue her but once the arms pulled her close against his frame, she knew it wasn't. The man was built but not as well built as the biceps she'd felt up not less than twenty minutes ago. The height was not quite Nate's but tall and slender just the same.

"Parker." Amelia prayed her smile did not display her disappointment. "You're here."

"I'm Sam's best man," said Parker. "And you are stunning."

The DJ slowed the tempo. Parker laced his fingers behind her lower back. Uncomfortable, Amelia rested her hands against his chest for space. "Thank you. You're looking pretty dapper yourself. Why didn't you attend the bachelor auction last week?"

"Would you have bought me?"

A crooked grin paused on her face. "Nate and I had some unfinished business."

Parker's smile matched hers. "Had? So now you're free for me?"

"Oh, Parker." Amelia sighed. "I don't want to go down this road with you."

"C'mon, what road?" Parker asked.

"I didn't come back in town to pick up where we left off."

"Which was with me watching you drive off into the sunset?"

If Amelia rolled her eyes one more time tonight, she was sure to lose an eyelash. "Parker."

"Amelia," he mocked, then grinned. He tugged her closer. "I'm playing with you. Anyone with eyes can see what's going on between you and Nate Reyes."

"What?"

"Don't play dumb with me, Amelia. You forget we shared our first kiss together."

"And preferably your last," said Nate's booming voice from behind Amelia.

Parker gave Amelia a quick wink and another squeeze.

"Nate Reyes," he said with a tight smile. "Here you are—again. Keeping away from the fires?"

"Oh, you know me," said Nate, reaching for Amelia's shoulders, "always trying to put them out when they need to be."

"Nate." Amelia cocked her head to the side.

"It's okay, Amelia," said Parker, letting her go. "I'll see you tomorrow. I'll have the DJ request our prom song if you'll save me a dance."

Not sure how to respond, Amelia shook her head and chuckled. As Parker disappeared into the crowd, Nate spun her around and pulled her into his arms. "You weren't nice."

"What?" he asked with a forced innocent twinkle in his green eyes. "I came down here to put out a fire."

Amelia cast a glance in the direction where Parker disappeared. "There's no fire between me and Parker."

"Clearly," Nate mumbled.

"What fire were you thinking of?"

"I understand Brittany is here." He sighed. "I didn't want her to make things uncomfortable."

"Uncomfortable for whom? Me? Or for you, when I leave?"

Nate scowled down at her. "Leave for where? You don't have a job, remember?"

"Perhaps not with MET." Amelia bit her lip. At this point in their relationship—whatever that meant—Amelia knew she needed to stop with her fabrication. In truth, she hadn't expected to hit things off with Nate outside of a bed. Getting to know him made it harder to face leaving at the end of the month. Grandmamma would be home Monday and Amelia gave herself a couple of weeks to get her settled into the new arrangements and then she'd head back on the *Azúcar* tour. Reality TV was her life. Southwood would never be as exciting.

So, recalling her plans to leave town in a week, she talked herself into keeping it to herself that she'd been suspended and not fired. She had something slick to say but any form of comment was lost in a gasp when Nate spun her around and dipped her. He held her body close to the ground, cradling her head and lower back.

"Let's not talk about the future," Nate whispered in her ear, "at least nothing after the next few hours."

Amelia's right brow rose in curiosity. "Only a few hours? Why, Nathaniel Reyes, I do declare," she said in her utmost Scarlett O'Hara imitation.

The rest of the evening blew by in a breeze. Nate held Amelia's hand the entire evening, dragging her with him through every joint-bachelorette-bachelor game possible from Never Have I Ever and the newlywed game to a good, old-fashioned soul-train line. Only couples were invited to hang out in the VIP section, and Nate was grateful for Sam and Emily playing Cupid. Instead each man pulled a slip of paper with a name on it from a top hat and then the women did the same. The names were all male characters from different movies. He guessed each movie was a romance. Nate drew the name Darius Lovehall. When Amelia sauntered over to him and displayed her name, Nina Mosley, he remembered the movie *Love Jones*. Not all couples were matched perfectly like they were but Nate didn't care. The prize for matching up the fastest was crowns for a king and queen, courtesy of Lexi and her shop. The winners also had the time to share a slow dance before the group left for a decked-out party bus to bring everyone home. Nate had been so sexually charged watching Amelia lick buttercream icing off her naughty-themed cupcake and sucking the lime after her tequila shot, he wasn't sure he'd be able to make it out of the bus.

"You didn't have to walk me to my door," said Amelia.

Nate took Amelia's house keys from her hand and shook his head as they walked up the ramp he'd built with his own two hands. "Of course I did."

"Afraid the bogeyman might be waiting?"

"If he goes by the name of Parker Ward." Nate grimaced. "Seems like he was everywhere tonight."

"Whatever."

Before sticking the key into the door, Nate turned to wink. "Hey, I'm pulling out all the stops here to make sure you're not planning on saving a dance with him tomorrow."

"I can't save a dance?"

"No," said Nate, trying to contain his desire as her airy giggle filled the night air. "You're to only save everything for me."

The bus's horn blew and took off, laughter echoing in the early morning hours. The passengers they'd partied with tonight hung out the window waving goodbye. If Nate didn't know any better, he was sure his brother was driving the bus.

"Your ride seems to have left you," said Amelia, nodding in the direction of the disappearing red taillights.

"Remind me to kill my brother tomorrow," Nate grumbled. He took her keys and opened the front door. "Mind if I use the phone to call a cab?"

Amelia batted her lashes and shook her head. "It's late, Nate. And it's not like you haven't spent the night here before."

"True." Nate cleared his throat. He opened the door with ease and stepped aside to allow her inside. When he reached to hand her the house keys, Amelia clasped her small, soft hand with his and gave him a sly smile as she pulled him through the doorway.

"But this will be the first night you sleep in my bed."

Not needing another word, Nate stepped farther inside and kicked the door closed with his foot. Amelia guided him through the living room to the stairs, occasionally giving him a seductive blink when she glanced over her shoulders. She took two steps before him and brought herself to his eye level.

Nate steadied himself as Amelia leaned forward to press her lips against his. Immediately he swiped his tongue into her sweet, frosting-flavored mouth. He increased the intensity of the kiss, wrapping his arms around her waist and pulling her against his hard body. Every inch of him ached for her. His fingers traced her heart-shaped derriere. Their tongues danced to the rhythm of their moans. Amelia's fingers traced his shoulders, his chest and the waistband of his pants. She fumbled with his belt buckle and he sighed with desire as the strap of leather hit the stairs. He was ready...so, so ready.

Desperate hands reached for the opening of her one-piece outfit. The swell of one breast was cupped in the palm of his hand. Nate's fingers twitched and in pent-up anticipation he reached for the opening of the top and yanked it open. The ampleness of her breasts made it hard to access them, so he pulled harder, ripping the material down to her belly button.

"Nate," she gasped into his ear with a delightful surprise.

"Sorry, not sorry," he replied before lowering her backside to the steps. His fingers skillfully pulled away the material of her bra, freeing her breasts with both hands and pressing them together. His mouth sought the peaks of the hard nipples he'd been craving since they first got together.

As his mouth fastened on both of them, Amelia clasped her legs around his waist and ground herself on him.

Amelia clawed at the hem of his shirt until she managed to pull the black material to his shoulders. Nate ceased feasting on her breasts enough to pull the shirt over his head. A ripple of pleasure spread across his body with the touch of her hands along his spine, around his collarbone and to his bare chest. A trail of heat followed her fingertips. He inhaled deeply when her fingers sunk below the fabric of his pants. She rounded her fingers to his backside and tugged the material. With the belt removed, the material came down with ease. Her hands reached under the waistband of his boxers and freed his straining erection.

"Amelia," he whispered between the valley of her breasts.

"Nate," she mocked. "Let's take this into my bedroom."

Without hesitation, Nate secured her bottom and stood upright with her legs wrapped around his waist. In the week he'd been here, he'd already learned his way around Helen Marlow's home, including where to find Amelia's new bedroom. He walked with ease and desire driving him. Their mouths never broke their kiss until he laid her on top of her white comforter.

Amelia rose to her elbows and shifted her body enough to allow him to free her of the rest of the flimsy material he'd torn away. As Nate pulled the last of the garment down her shapely legs, he held her foot in his hand and kissed her ankles, then the arch. She pulled her leg in, bending it at the knee, thus pulling him close. Nate knelt on the edge of the bed and held both legs out to the side. His fingers read her inner thigh like braille until he came to the center of her core.

With the pad of his thumb and forefinger, he massaged her outer lips, rubbing them together. Hot, liquid moisture coated his fingers. Slowly he sunk one finger into her flesh. Her upper body rose off the bed. Nate, not wanting to break his concentration, eased her back down onto the mattress by circling her left nipple with the palm of his hand.

Nate drove his finger deeper into her wet flesh and pulled out. He did it again, deeper, and let his thumb trace circles on her throbbing nub. A cry escaped Amelia's throat as she began to quiver. His body trembled, knowing how ready she was for him. He sighed at the view and swallowed down his desire. The pads of his thumbs traced the delicate skin of her inner thigh. Her hands pawed the air toward his chest, willing him to come closer. He obliged.

Two full weeks had passed since he'd last touched her body, with a week of her teasing him with visions of her sexy body. But not tonight—he could no longer wait.

"I need you," Amelia whispered. She arched her neck and turned her head to the side as she thrust her lower back toward him.

In seconds Nate kicked off his pants, rolled on a condom from his wallet in the back of his pants and joined her naked body with his, entering her swiftly. They both sighed, clearly satisfied with the reunion. Her tight walls clamped around his shaft. He closed his eyes and tried to maintain stability.

Amelia gasped in satisfaction. Nate nuzzled his mouth against the crook of her neck and began to lick and suck. Her fingernails scratched the length of his back. Not wanting to come too soon, Nate held Amelia's hands over her head and drove into her. Like the first time they were together, she matched his thrusts with one of her own. They were a perfect fit. They moved in harmony. Nate dipped his head lower and captured her mouth with his. The tongues danced again to the sound of their bodies pounding against each other. Nate let go of Amelia's hands and balanced himself on his own hands to watch her face as he drove into her over and over. As her back arched in anticipation of another orgasm, Nate drove faster. The moment her eyes tightened, he let go of his pent-up desire with a yelp, thrusting until he was spent.

He could never find bliss like this with anyone else.

Chapter 9

The elegance of the Keaton-Marshall wedding almost made Amelia want to get married. *Almost.*

As promised, Amelia helped out Lexi's employee, Chantal, with the video. She was quite impressed with the amount of money Lexi had invested in her quality cameras. Amelia's fingers itched to take control but she let the young woman handle everything. She made mental notes of how she'd do things differently. She might have placed a GoPro camera on the baseball caps of the groomsmen from Sam's fraternity. Maybe next time, she could talk Lexi into getting some battery-pack microphones for the next bridal party to better catch all the conversations.

Next time? Amelia gave her head a little shake as she jotted her notes in the small notepad she kept in her handbag. There'd be no next time. After Grandmamma came home, Amelia would be around for a few more weeks and then she was out of here. Hell, wanting to hold a boom mic was proof she needed to get back to work.

"You look like you're in your element." Nate's deep voice vibrated against her spine as he snuck up behind her and wrapped his arms around her waist.

A slow smile spread across her face at the memory of Nate just a few hours ago. She'd thought that after staying up all night making love to him, she'd be tired by now, but at the moment of his touch she was recharged with desire. "I am now."

Out of view from everyone, Nate's hand snaked around to her backside and roamed across the curve of her behind. "Admit it, life is better *living* reality than *filming* it."

Amused with the idea, Amelia half nodded and half shook her head. "I've been doing film for a while now. I've only been doing you for a couple of hours."

"And already you're contemplating staying," he retorted.

Had he read her thoughts? No, not possible. Amelia shook her head and spun around. With Nate's arms still on her body, she was flush against his chest. The pale lavender scoop-necked tea-length dress Lexi's niece had picked out for her crushed against Nate's dark suit, pressing her breasts forward and drawing Nate's attention to them.

"You believe one night of passion can…" Whatever she wanted to say was drowned out in the back of her throat when Nate dipped his head lower and kissed her. The sweetness of his mouth made her knees buckle. Thank God for his hold.

"Are you crazy?" she asked breathlessly. "Anyone can see us."

Nate shrugged without a care in the world as they stood in the back of the church. Maybe there was something in the water. All the other couples they'd hung out with last night were cuddled up. Stephen snatched Lexi's clipboard from her hand and drew her close for a kiss. Cay and Greg slipped out from the church to the hallway connected to the back room for a few stolen kisses. "Is something in the water?"

"The pastor's running late, so we all have a few minutes to misbehave."

As she prayed that the pastor going missing during a wedding was not a bad omen, Amelia sunk into Nate's embrace and enjoyed the moment.

During the wedding, she took a quiet seat in the back pew away from prying eyes. As nice as Emily and Sam were for extending an olive branch to her, Amelia did not trust the elders who had been affected by her exposé on the peach tree famers to not have something negative to say during the wedding.

Amelia didn't get another chance to enjoy Nate's touch until after the vows were sealed with a kiss and the wedding party was on its way to where the reception started. The reception was held in Down Park, the area connecting all four bordering counties. A white gazebo shaded the guests from the grueling late-summer heat and any threat of rain. Guests sat on white wooden folding chairs at the twelve-top royal-purple-and-cream themed tables. Everyone who was anyone was attending the event. Apart from Brittany Foley, Amelia did not receive the hate she expected. The bridesmaid shot as many daggers as she possibly could at Amelia during the wedding but Amelia didn't care. She was on cloud nine, dancing with Nate.

"For the record," Nate said as he twirled Amelia around, "the girls adore you."

Amelia glanced over at the table where Kimber, Nate's sixteen-year-old niece, sat under the watchful eye of Stephen Reyes, having turned down an offer to dance with one of the boys in attendance. "Is she shy?"

"No," Nate scoffed, "she's just grounded."

"For how long?"

Nate shrugged his shoulders. "How long before the end of time?"

Amelia winced for the girl and understood her pain. "Poor kid."

"Poor kid? My brother had a full head of hair before we moved here."

"What?"

"Joking." Nate winked and tightened his grip around her waist. "How long before we can leave here?"

"They haven't even cut the cake, Nate." Though she wanted to be the mature one in this scenario, Amelia knew her desire mirrored his. How did a suit make a man so sexy? It didn't matter what Nate wore: a pair of denims with no shirt and the sweat off his back, or a dark, tailored suit. She inhaled deeply. She'd already missed the county fair, which was always held at the beginning of the summer, but she pictured him in a nice green sweater to match his eyes in the winter months or even an orange shirt for pumpkin patch season. The farmers were probably tending feverishly to their crops now, given that Halloween wasn't too far away from here. Hell, September was a few days away. And then what? She'd report back to work? Maybe she could stay at least through next month.

"You okay?"

"I'm fine," she said. *More than fine*, she thought, with a new plan in mind now. She'd give Rory Montgomery a call later on this weekend and let her know.

For the first time in a long time, Nate realized bringing a date to a wedding was not complicated at all. For once he liked the feeling of being in a secluded relationship. Is that what they were? Secluded? The idea brought a smile to his face.

"I'll have whatever you're having," said an elderly gentleman stepping up to the bar next to Nate.

"Nothing but tonic water for me," Nate said, raising his glass, and turned. His grin widened at the sight of Enzo Gravel, Kimber and Philly's grandfather. Earlier this year Betty's parents had made the heartbreaking decision not to file for custody of their granddaughters. Nate's brother, Ken, had made the arrangements for Stephen and Nate to be the girls' guardians after each birth. No one expected Ken and Betty to die, but Nate and Stephen had the courts on their side. Enzo and his wife, Jeanette, admitted they were too old to run after the younger girls. They'd had Betty in their midforties and were pushing the seventies when their first grandchild was born. Now in their eighties they did what most grandparents did and spoiled their kids every chance they had with them, without having the responsibility of disciplining them.

"Hey, man." Nate extended his hand. "I didn't see you there."

"Ah, that must be the young lady you've been dancing with the whole evening?" He gave Nate a firm handshake. The kind of shake his father, Esteban, had taught him. "Who is the lucky lady?"

"Amelia Marlow."

Enzo tapped the white goatee on the chin of his mahogany face. "Where do I know the name?"

"You may remember her. Her parents owned—"

"The Scoop, an ice-cream parlor off Main Street. Yes, I remember Amelia. Inquisitive young lady."

His choice in words caused Nate to chuckle, especially as he recalled the way she always tried different angles of getting to the truth about Stephen's meeting with Natalia. Nate had stood firm on his word. If Natalia wanted to share with Amelia that she was ready to leave the business, then it was Natalia's story to tell. Nate loved Amelia, but not enough to betray his friends and family. *Wait—love?*

"Amelia did the city a whole lot of good," Enzo went on. "Although what a shame she didn't stick around to see what good she did."

Over many of their conversations, Amelia often chalked her reason for not wanting to return to Southwood up to everyone here hating her. So far, except Brittany for obvious reasons, everyone seemed to be so friendly. She'd never said why she felt they hated her, other than they did. Nate took a swig of his water as Enzo went on.

"Amelia was investigating the issue of how migrant workers were treated in Peachville. Initially, her high-school report ruffled a lot of feathers."

"Why?"

"This is Georgia, son. The peach tree is our everything. If I'm not mistaken, the initial findings halted the harvesting and put a lot of businesses in the red, including her family's shop." Enzo closed his eyes and let out a sigh of nostalgia. "Man, what I wouldn't do for a scoop of her father's fresh peach ice cream."

What Nate wouldn't do for a bite of her peach. Libido racing, Nate glanced at his watch and wondered how long they needed to stay. Neither of them were a part of the wedding party, so they did not have to stay for photographs. Nate cleared his throat. "So, are the girls going home with you tonight?"

"Philly asked."

"And Kimber?" asked Nate. With him being gone all week, Nate had worried about Stephen handling his time with the girls and was grateful for Lexi being around. A feminine presence was necessary in the household and while Stephen and Lexi were not married or engaged, it was only a matter of time. Nate typically enjoyed his nights off and away from the household to socialize. Having the grandparents take the girls for the weekend helped Nate avoid *the talk* with his nieces. Before Amelia, there'd been no desire to introduce the girls to whomever kept him company.

"She wanted to know if she'd still be grounded if she came over," Enzo said, giving Nate a wink and a nudge in the rib cage to jar him out of his thoughts, "but you guys know Jeanette and I always follow your rules."

"Sure." Nate returned the wink. "Which is why I have a tracker on all of her phones. She can try and go out with her friends, but I'll be watching. I should have weighed Philly this morning."

"Now you can't blame the sugar on me today. Philly's been eyeballing that six-tier cake all afternoon. You should have all week," said Enzo, "but from my understanding you haven't been home much."

Not sure how to answer the question, Nate shook his head. "Well, you see…" He still did not have a proper answer. How did he explain their meeting in Atlanta or what happened when Amelia returned to Southwood?

"Save your excuses," Enzo said with a chuckle. "I am hard of hearing, not hard of hearing gossip."

"Gossip?" Nate's jaws clenched. If Amelia got wind of that, she might hightail it back to the reality TV world.

"Don't worry." Enzo waved off any fret. "Pastor Rivers informed me of the work you're doing for Helen Marlow. Bless your soul, have you met her yet?"

"Briefly."

"And you're still living?"

The memory of her prickly demeanor did bring a chuckle to Nate. "Yes, sir."

"Good for you. Well, looks like my blushing bride is waving me over."

Enzo nodded and shook Nate's hand before excusing himself to rejoin his wife at a table filled with other pillars of the community. Nate's green eyes scanned the gazebo for any sight of Amelia and found her in the arms of Parker Ward—again. He took a step toward the laid-out dance floor and over the greenery of the park.

"Dance with me."

The latest obstacle to get in Nate's way was the five-foot-five bridesmaid dressed in purple and accented with jealousy green. "Hello, Brit. I'm in a bit of a hurry."

"Dance with me," Brittany repeated like one of Philly's broken dolls. She glanced over her shoulder. "She seems pretty busy catching up with her first love."

She'd voiced what he'd already suspected. Nate shrugged his shoulders. "So?"

Brittany reached for Nate's hand and dragged him to the edge of the dance floor. At least he'd be a few steps closer to Amelia.

"I'm disappointed in you, Nate." Brittany stated the obvious.

"Why?" Nate tried not to sigh. Other wedding guests began to crowd the floor, causing Brittany to get closer. In turn, Parker was probably trying the same move.

"You've been ignoring me."

"Correct me if I'm wrong—" Nate cleared his throat "—but we never made each other any promises."

Brittany's fingers, with their purple acrylic nails, walked their way up the buttons of his shirt. "We've always had an unspoken bond between us."

"Brittany, please," he begged before she humiliated herself. Philly craned her neck to watch them dance. She was always hinting around for Nate to invite her favorite teacher home for dinner. "Stop."

"You forgot already?"

"Forgot what?" Nate jerked his head away from her approaching face.

"The safe word."

The one time Brittany had gone into the padlocked room at her apartment, she'd mentioned something about a safe word. How the hell did she expect him to remember? Jaws twitching with irritation, Nate inhaled deeply and glanced around the dance floor and made eye contact with Amelia. Instead of the pissed-off glare he expected, she winked with confidence, almost as if she found amusement in his predicament.

"Did you forget the safe word, Nate?"

Nate ducked his head out of her grasp before she placed her dominatrix fingers on his chin to force his attention. "Brittany, I told you I don't do—"

"Complicated." Brittany motioned with her hands in front of his face with air quotes. "Yes, yes, I understand you have a family to take care of and an image you want to uphold for your nieces, which is why I am the logical choice. No one has suspected our relationship so far with all the parent-teacher meetings."

Making a turn on the floor, Nate shook his head. "You've made yourself pretty damn clear to every single woman in town."

"And not so single," Brittany mocked.

"Things are more complicated," he said honestly.

"You've said something along those lines before."

"And every time I meant it." He kept his lips straight to show seriousness. Brittany made the small things uncomfortable. There hadn't been a school function where she didn't cling to his arm, silently laying claim to him amongst all the other single mothers.

"You also said you did not believe in bringing dates to

weddings." Brittany nodded her chin in Amelia's direction. "Or did something change?"

"You mean someone?" Nate asked. His harsh stare down at Brittany softened. She didn't deserve to be set on the curb but he'd never made her any promises. In fact, Nate made himself perfectly clear: he was not looking for anything serious from her.

A murmur of conversation spread through the dance floor as the song began to wind down. Nate's heart rate sped up. He turned at the right moment—to witness Amelia departing Parker's arms. She made her way toward him. Automatically Nate's arms dropped from Brittany's waist.

"Hi, guys."

At the sound of Amelia's cheery voice, the corners of Brittany's eyes narrowed. Her crow's-feet deepened and anger flashed in her eyes when she turned to him. "You say you don't do complicated, but sure seems as though you'll settle for easy."

Before either of them got a word out of their mouths, Brittany stormed off toward the table where her grandfather, Pastor Rivers, sat nursing a bottle of water. In true dramatic flair, Amelia clutched her heart. "Did I say something wrong?" she gasped playfully.

Nate shook his hand and captured hers. "You're so wrong."

"Wrong for what?"

The next song started, an Alabama Shakes bluesy tune filtering through the air. "For stealing the show."

"I'm not doing anything but enjoying this reception."

"The bride is supposed to be the center of attention," said Nate, "and here you've got all eyes on you right now."

Amelia batted her lashes, and though he knew she was playing up her flippant side, he'd learned she did this a lot when she became uncomfortable. "Whatever. More like everyone is staring at you." Her hands pressed against the lapels of his jacket.

"How much longer do you want to stay here?"

"We can leave now."

They stayed long enough to watch the bride and groom cut the cake and smear a piece across one another's faces. Grateful that Enzo and Jeanette had offered to take the girls tonight, Nate bid his nieces good-night. Philly whined a bit but the wheels in Kimber's mind had begun turning. Pastor Rivers tipped his head in their direction, trying to get either his or Amelia's attention, but with what Nate had in mind to do with Amelia, the last person he wanted to talk to was a man of the cloth.

Lexi was an obstacle in Nate and Amelia's attempted departure. She wanted to be sure she had Amelia's notes written down on what to film and what angle to take the footage at for Sam and Emily. Outside, another issue slowed them down. All the cars driving aimlessly around trying to find a spot made getting to his SUV seem more like a game of Frogger. Keenan, Stephen's part-time driver, offered to take them wherever, but again, Nate wasn't sure he was going to make it all the way back to Amelia's without ripping off her clothes. He surely did not need an employee of Stephen's to watch.

Once again Nate drove down County Road Seventeen like a madman, one hand on the wheel while the other pulled her body close to him for a kiss. Amelia thought she might actually burst into flames if she did not touch every inch of Nate's body. For a moment he lost control of the wheel when she yanked open the buttons of his shirt and exposed the tribal tattoo. His tires skidded off the road with each devilish kiss Amelia trailed across his neck, down his chest and against his hard abs. The steering wheel needed to be adjusted to accommodate what she planned on doing to Nate. Her fingers fought feverishly at the button of his slacks until she released him and took him in her mouth.

"Amelia," Nate breathed nervously.

Loving the way his body tensed up, Amelia smiled and slid her mouth down the length of his shaft. His breath became shallow and she took him in deeper. Three of her fingers barely managed to wrap around the base and moved up and down with a slight release of the pressure of her mouth. She loved hearing him call her name over and over.

With the use of his right hand, Nate slid his fingers down the hem of her dress and began to lift the material up. She was so glad she was wearing a pair of thigh-highs. His thumb traced the lace on her thigh and his stomach moved with his chuckle.

"Woman, you are the devil."

To show him how much of a devil she could be, Amelia swirled the tip of her tongue around the slick head of his penis and jerked her hand upward, milking out the droplets of precum. "Am I now?"

The answer to her question was a thrust of his long finger between the flesh at the apex of her legs. She'd been wet all afternoon and purred once she finally received his touch. They moved rhythmically in unison to the beat of the song on the radio. By the time the car crunched over the gravel driveway, Amelia was saturated with desire.

Nate threw his SUV in Park and snatched out the keys. He trotted in front of the hood to the passenger's side and opened the door. Amelia greeted him with one leg propped up on the cushioned seat, exposing herself for him. She adored the way he gulped and glanced around. Dusk began to settle on the dark treetops. Everyone who was anyone was at the wedding. No one could see them for miles.

The work she'd done on him was still evident. Amelia took her other leg and pressed it against his sculpted abs. Nate shrugged out of his jacket. The shirt she tore open had no way to stay closed and that suited her just fine. His pants hung low off his hips.

"I don't think I can wait until we get inside, Nate." Amelia bit the bottom right corner of her lip and blinked innocently.

"I don't like to make a woman have to wait."

Nate reconnected his body with hers first with a kiss. His hands clasped around the base of her neck and his fingers sunk into her curls. Their mouths danced to the orchestra of the cicadas. Nate skillfully rolled a condom on right before Amelia moved her lower half closer to the edge of the seat and slipped herself onto him with ease.

They both breathed a sigh of satisfaction.

"Is this what you've been waiting for?" Nate asked, moving inside her. He pulled his mouth from hers. The bold gaze of his deep green eyes shook her soul.

"Yes," Amelia managed to say. Her walls began to throb and suction with each thrust. She wanted to play it cool but the pleasure of his mouth on her breasts overtook her. She leaned back and allowed him to throw her four-inch lavender heels onto the green lawn and hook her legs over his shoulders and pound away. And at the right moment, the precise time he sent her over the edge, Nate's body tensed and his cock thumped against her womb. Amelia closed her eyes and rode the pleasure wave before she felt the cabin of the SUV begin to spin. Not able to look at him just yet, Amelia turned her head to the right and covered her face with her left arm. A small juice box caught her eye. Dear Lord Jesus, she realized this was the same vehicle he drove his nieces around in.

"We've violated your car," Amelia said with a giggle. *Since when did she giggle?*

"You say violate," Nate said breathily, "I say christened. And damn," he added. "I also say damn."

"You're crazy."

"And starving," he said. "Woman, you've worked an appetite out of me."

Nate helped her out of the front seat, adjusting the hem of her dress before tucking himself away and zipping up his pants. Amelia sighed in disappointment.

"Well, perhaps if you didn't spend the entire reception dancing with Brittany Foley." She began to laugh, then gasped with another fit of giggles when Nate tossed her over his broad shoulders with one arm and carried her toward the house. Instead of taking the steps to the front porch, he took her up the new ramp, hidden by Grandmamma's flowers. Before they made it to the porch, Nate let her down, turned her so she faced the wall and lifted the hem of her dress—then they christened the new ramp.

By the time they made it inside the house, Amelia was famished, as well. Thankfully she remembered the leftover Chinese food. The day before they'd picked up some take-out and Amelia had purposely ordered a dozen egg rolls, positive she'd eat at least two with her meal. Nate had polished off two before she transferred their rice onto a plate and had eaten still another with his meal. Those remaining called her name. The motor of the refrigerator went off when she opened the door to take out the red-lidded containers. Her stomach rumbled so loud she doubted she'd be able to wait until the microwave—a luxury item she'd tucked away in the corner of the counter—heated the rest of the egg rolls. *What! Only five left?* Math might not have been her strong suit but she could've sworn they had only had five the first night. Did Nate eat two for breakfast? She gave Nate a side-eye glance and wondered where he put the calories.

In the kitchen, she and Nate worked side by side, moving in unison. Without words, she ducked when he opened a cabinet and he stepped out of the way when she opened the oven. Once, Amelia had filmed in a fast-paced kitchen and enjoyed the dance of the chefs. She was reminded of them when she observed Nate and herself right now.

"I'm glad you decided to reheat the egg rolls in the oven," said Nate, leaning his long, lean body against the counter. His slacks still hung off his hips and his shirt was unbuttoned. "The crust will be crispier."

"I figured as much." Amelia sighed and nodded her head at the black microwave with the bright turquoise digital numbers counting down as a timer for the oven. "I wonder if buying this was a mistake. Grandmamma will never use it."

"I'm surprised she doesn't have one already." Nate folded his arms across his chest. His biceps flexed. Amelia wondered if it was possible to christen the kitchen in the ten minutes set for the oven.

"Because Grandmamma doesn't strike you as a patient woman?" Amelia smarted off.

"Leave my friend alone," Nate teased. "Let's find something else to do while we wait for the timer to go off."

Amelia's left brow rose in inquiry. "For eight minutes? Why, Mr. Reyes," she said in her Southern drawl, "you disappoint me."

Before the smirk fully spread across her face, Nate once again tossed her over his shoulder and headed up the stairs. Amelia squealed with laughter and feigned being a damsel in distress, loving every minute of his hard, muscular body manhandling her. When was the last time she'd had this much fun with a man?

"No one can save you now." Nate went along with the bit. He made his way up the stairs, careful of her head as he turned the corners to get to her bedroom.

Hanging upside down, Amelia reached for her brass doorknob and pushed the door closed seconds before Nate tossed her on the bed. Her stomach quivered with desire. Nate touched her toes and gave them a little squeeze. Amelia leaned up on her elbows and spread her legs, inviting him inside. A deep breath lodged in her throat just before he entered her. The breath turned into a startled gasp as someone pounded on her door.

"Is it me—" Nate leaned his body against hers "—or are we interrupted every time we make love in a bed?"

"Just half the time." Amelia covered her face with her hands. The pounding continued before she realized it wasn't her bedroom door being knocked on, but the stairs. *What the hell?*

"Amelia," Grandmamma's voice called out. "Is that you up there? I know you don't have a boy up in the room with you."

Chapter 10

The last time Nate had been forced to hide for a woman was a few weeks ago, moments before Amelia had opened the door to her angry colleague. Now he sat at his dining room table with his leg propped up, his knee sore from landing too hard on it after scaling down Amelia Marlow's bathroom window. It was a wonder he didn't break his neck, but he didn't want to have his neck broken by Helen Marlow. So far, the woman with the ornery reputation liked him and he wanted to stay in her good graces.

"You're not fifteen anymore." Stephen frowned, coming in from the kitchen with a fresh pack of ice.

"You don't say?" Nate responded and accompanied that with an eye roll. He'd hobbled into his SUV and made his way home in time to catch Lexi slinking out of the house he shared with his brother. Though he'd checked in on his nieces every day for their first week of school, he still felt like he hadn't been home in months. He missed the cotton-candy smell of Philly's clothes folded neatly in a white plastic laundry basket. He missed stumbling across the array of Kimber's colorful cell phones. Even though he'd agreed to allow Jeanette and Enzo to take the girls with them overnight, a part of him regretted it. Walking through the doors and not being attacked by hugs and kisses made him feel strangely empty.

"What kind of example are you setting for the girls?" Stephen continued to lecture.

Nate sat up farther in the high-back chair to accept the freezing bag. He pulled up the hem of his red basketball shorts and rested the bag over his knee where the skin displayed a bright red, puffy sight. "The girls are with Jeanette and Enzo."

"And how long do you plan on sneaking around?"

Nate wasn't sure where his brother was going with this. "What?" His eyebrows rose.

"You were able to tell the girls last week the reason you were gone was because of the commitment you made for the bachelor auction."

Nate raised his pointer finger in the air. "An auction you *volunteered* me for."

"I didn't volunteer you to spend the nights at her place."

"Well," Nate said, shrugging his shoulders, "as I explained to the girls already, I slept in the barn."

"Fine, but your job with Amelia is done. Now what?" Stephen took a seat opposite his brother. "Her grandmother is back from the hospital."

"I'm not going to disrespect her grandmother's house, if you're worried about that," said Nate, toying with a stray piece of wicker from the basket on the center of the table.

A bowl of fruit sat on the table before him—one of Lexi's influences. Prior to her coming, their table usually had pizza boxes stacked on it. In fact, the dining room at

Amelia's grandmother's place reminded him of their pre-Lexi days. From what he'd learned of Amelia, he knew she stayed busy. Now that she didn't have a job, would she become more domesticated? He'd hoped hanging out with her old friends would inspire her to stay. Lexi utilizing Amelia's skills as a videographer was genius. He hoped that when he met up with Amelia later on today she'd be excited about putting together the footage for Sam and Emily. He wished she'd want to stay. And then what?

"The whole reason Amelia came back to Southwood was to take care of her grandmother. What happens when she leaves?" Stephen's question reiterated Nate's thoughts. "Before she came, you were going through the women in town."

"I haven't gone through all the women."

"Not all." Stephen nodded. "But you've gone through enough of them, telling them to back away because you *don't do complicated.*" Stephen made air quotes with his hands. "You've been running through the women, leaving all of them thinking you might take them as your date for Sam's wedding."

"Give me a break, big brother." Nate sighed and shook his head. "I never once gave any of the ladies I've dated—"

"Dated?" Stephen interrupted with a raised brow and another set of air quotes.

"I never gave them the inkling I wanted to take anyone to the wedding. I didn't think I'd want to attend."

"Until you met Amelia?"

"I thought you liked Amelia?" asked Nate.

"Amelia is great, but you've felt this need to cover for her because you got her fired."

"I'm not covering for her," said Nate. "I'm trying to get her to find a reason to stay in town."

"So you two can what? Sneak around?"

"Date." The usually awkward word rolled off Nate's lips with ease. True, he'd never committed himself to one single lady, but he wanted to give it a try with Amelia. The idea of dating Amelia didn't scare him, but rather relaxed him. This seemed natural.

Stephen paused his lecture to cock his head to the side. "You said she was fired, Nate." Stephen shook his head and pressed his hands against the table. "She doesn't have a job."

Nate shrugged his shoulders, biting back the ounce of pain he'd gotten from brushing up against the brick wall in his attempt to hide from Helen Marlow. *"Yet,"* he corrected his brother. "Amelia doesn't have a job yet and the lease on her apartment is almost up. This is perfect timing."

"You're going to take her on as a client?"

Part of Reyes Realty and Contracting meant selling homes. The brothers were so successful in their business back in Atlanta that they'd been able to concentrate on their nieces without having to worry about work and clients. Nate was good at selling and finding dream homes for people. He preferred the hands-on part when they flipped homes.

Stephen gave a skeptical clearing of his throat. "So you think you're enough to keep her here?"

"Amelia's grandmother is here, and her cousin."

"From my understanding, her grandmother doesn't like too many people, her granddaughter included."

Shaking his head, Nate chuckled. "Haven't you learned your lesson listening to rumors?"

"We're talking about you, little brother."

"Whatever."

"No, not whatever." Stephen's voice became sterner, reminding Nate of their father moments before he laid down the law. "Let's talk about the next week or so Amelia is in town. How do you plan on conducting yourself with Kimber and Philly in the house?"

"I'm going to start off with inviting Amelia over for dinner, hang out with us so she'll see the perks of staying in town, and then I'm bringing her to the Crystal Coquí Ball."

Stephen choked on his words. "What? I don't understand."

"Don't worry," Nate replied with a smug grin, "it's not too complicated."

Amelia spent Sunday afternoon pretty much how she did when she lived with Grandmamma—in her room. She wanted to avoid the pressures and questions from the few church patrons who stopped by with a covered dish. After she'd practically pushed Nate out the window, Amelia had gone downstairs to say hello to the visitors and make sure she did not get *the eye* from Grandmamma. She took to the top steps and eavesdropped on Grandmamma bragging about the new ramp Nate Reyes had put in for her. Occasionally she heard the screen door squeak for Grandmamma to show off. The ladies who came to visited hummed and prayed in thanks for a man like Nate Reyes. Their form of thankful prayer might have turned more into gossip about the time each of the ladies caught a glimpse of Nate playing basketball down at the park with their own grandchildren, or running into him at the store. According to what Amelia learned from the church ladies, domestication made Nate sexy as hell.

Twenty-four hours later Grandmamma still did not mention anything about Nate sneaking out of the house, but so as to not borrow trouble, Amelia took off the moment Grandmamma asked for a new bag of ice. Amelia guessed her friends drank all the iced tea. Besides, getting out of the house felt liberating. A few days ago, Amelia had wanted to spend her time in Southwood hiding, since she'd been too afraid of running into anyone. But thanks to talking to folks at Emily's wedding, Amelia had learned her senior exposé had done more good to the community than harm. Too bad she didn't plan to stick around to find out how people's attitude to her had changed.

The black cell phone in her purse came to life as Amelia pulled into the Piggly Wiggly parking lot and put her car in Park. When she answered her phone, she thought she might have sung her greeting. Her toes wiggled in the jeweled flip-flops on her feet.

"Well, someone sure is in a good mood."

"Rory," Amelia exclaimed, tucking a strand of hair behind her ear to better hear. "How are you?"

"I'm fine." Rory laughed into the receiver. "Small-town life is treating you well?"

A shiver ran down Amelia's spine. The temperature had crept up to eighty-five degrees and it was only eight thirty in the morning. One man made being back in town better. "Life back home is not as bad as I thought."

"Does any of this have to do with a particular man?"

Amelia cleared her throat. "I'm not kissing and telling."

"At least I know you're kissing," Rory quipped. "Listen here, missy, I know Christopher said you're not allowed to contact anyone in the business but you did not have to leave a message on *my* work phone. I heard your message this morning, and before I get mad at you for not calling me at home, how's your grandmother?"

"Grandmamma?" Amelia shook her head back and forth. "She's fine," she started off with a slow drawl and filled her friend in on the updates and remodeling.

"Good grief, there *is* a man," guessed Rory. "The same one you purchased?"

"How'd you know?"

"Natalia demanded to speak to the higher-ups before she took off."

"Took off?" Amelia scratched her head. A teenager zipped by on a skateboard in front of the automatic doors, triggering the signal for them to open. "What do you mean, took off?"

"She's took off and left everyone in Atlanta."

A thousand questions ran through Amelia's mind. "Where did she go? Is she okay? What's going on with the show?"

"Postponed for now. The rest of the family went back to their island home in Puerto Rico."

"And the crew?" The pause on the other end of the line indicated trouble. Amelia let out a whistle. While MET paid their employees well, a lot of bonuses were given to the camera crew if they were able to catch a scandalous conversation or an outrageous act from one of the family members. The camera loved Natalia, but the female public loved her brother Nicholas and often tried to get him in precarious situations. Twitter had been his downfall. Nicholas's bad habit of wanting to let everyone know where he was going often led to a swarm of women waiting to throw themselves at him. The Nicholas crew earned bonuses for every half-naked woman they caught sneaking out of his hotel room.

Amelia imagined Rory shaking her head back and forth. "Nope, you know Christopher does not want you to think about work while you're on leave. Are you ready to come back to work?"

Considering Grandmamma was getting better, Amelia could go back to work, but the image of Nate's face flashed in her mind. He wasn't out of her system.

"Your hesitation tells me you want to extend your stay,"

said Rory. "We've got an assistant producer on standby in case Natalia shows up, so you're free to continue your leave."

"How mad would Mr. Kelly be?"

Rory sighed on the other end of the line. "He's fine with however much time you want to take. Jesus, girl, you haven't taken a break since you started here. Chris didn't think four weeks was going to be enough. Wait until I tell him."

"Don't tell him everything," Amelia said, panicked.

"I'll tell him—" Rory faked a cough into the receiver "—you're sick or something."

Laughing, Amelia shook her head. "You're supposed to be a professional at a multibillion-dollar company."

"Yes, but I'm your friend first. Take as much time as you need."

"It's not like I'm never coming back." Amelia chewed on her bottom lip; her mind wondered what Natalia was up to. First she'd had a secret meeting with an old friend and now this disappearing act. Her fingers itched to call up Natalia.

"Famous last words," Rory sang before she ended the call.

After hanging up with her friend, Amelia stepped out of her grandmother's Nissan and pulled up the elastic of her black yoga pants before she headed inside the convenience store. Amelia had turned in her rental yesterday afternoon with Pastor Rivers, who volunteered to give her a ride back to the house. It seems since he was the one who found Grandmamma, he'd driven her car to the hospital and had hung on to it until Grandmamma was better.

Amelia let out a sigh with the relief of the pressure of her waistband. All this eating out was putting a damper on her figure. Amelia folded her arms over her faded green, over-washed Florida A&M T-shirt and stood in front of the rack filled with tabloids and glossy magazines with celebrities on the covers. With her forced break from work, she had somewhat lost touch with life in the reality TV world. Two weeks ago, the coverage of the Ruiz family had been crazy. The family had been featured in every magazine. There was no such thing as bad publicity. Rather than every tabloid magazine featuring Natalia and her family, just every other magazine did. However, instead of catching Natalia in some risqué pose or gown, a question mark covered her face. *Have you seen her?* captioned the photos.

Amelia grabbed three magazines and a bag of ice and headed to the register. To avoid her name being recognized by the cashier—a man she remembered being in detention a lot during high school—Amelia paid for her purchases with cash and headed for a quick exit. The sliding glass doors dinged her departure. A group of teenagers skateboarded off the curb of the walkway in front of the convenience store. Despite the temperatures spiking into triple digits, some of the boys wore knit caps over their heads. She shook her head and chuckled, biting back the irony of the boys' flip-flops.

"I'd be careful of smiling like that."

"What?" Amelia's attention was drawn to the hot guy leaning against the hood of her grandmother's car. Her heart skipped a beat at the sight of Nate in a pair of black basketball shorts, a T-shirt and a pair of athletic slides covering his bare feet. With his arms folded across his chest, she got a peek at the tattoo peeping out from the V of his shirt. She pressed her lips together to keep from smiling too hard.

"Your smile is capable of melting your bag of ice." Nate pushed away from her car to meet her. He took the bag from her hand, letting his thumb stroke across her wrist. Her heart raced. "Let me get this."

"Are you stalking me?" Amelia teased. She tucked the magazines under her arm for fear of being ridiculed.

"If I am?" He took her keys from her other hand and walked toward the trunk.

Amelia cocked her head to the side and enjoyed the view. "I'm not complaining."

"So I've caught you in a good mood?"

"You're the second person to point out my demeanor. Am I normally a grouch?"

Nate winked. "I'm not answering the question on grounds I'm planning on kissing you later."

With a playful groan, Amelia rolled her eyes. "I'm in a good mood because I'm out of the house."

"Did your grandmother find evidence of me being there and threaten to ground you?" Nate opened and shut the trunk and joined Amelia as she leaned against the door of the driver's side of her vehicle. Nate had parked his SUV next to hers and stood with his back to his passenger door and his feet stretched toward hers.

"No, she hasn't mentioned you being there—" Amelia cringed at the next thought "—which only leads me to believe she was already in the house when we returned because she didn't block your car in the driveway."

With a low whistle, Nate shook his head. "We didn't do anything in the house."

A flash of what they did do flared against the pit of her stomach. "No, there was the incident in the car."

Nate tossed a glance off his shoulder. A slow smile spread across his face. "Yeah, but that side of the door faced the woods."

"And the ramp?" Amelia reminded him. The bay window sat right above the spot where they'd wickedly made love. Grandmamma may have had a bird's-eye view of the whole event—which made her wonder why she didn't mention it this morning.

Nate's clearing of his throat brought Amelia out of her mortification. "We need to not have this conversation."

"About where my grandmother may have spied us having sex?"

"Yes."

"Why?"

"Because—" Nate closed the gap between them "—all this sex talk is arousing me. I've got these ballers on and there's a group of teenage boys I'd rather not have see me go with a full-on adolescent, uncontrollable boner."

"What?" Amelia keeled over with laughter.

"Great, making fun of me now?"

"I'm sorry," she said, trying to cover her mouth to keep from laughing. One of the magazines slipped and they both reached for it, knocking their heads at the same time. Nate clasped Amelia's shoulders. His eyes scanned the cover and his brows rose with concern.

"Are you okay?" he asked softly.

"I'm fine." More than a twinge of guilt racked Amelia's frame at his concern. Nate felt guilty for getting her fired—or at least he was still under the impression she'd given him. Why didn't she let him off the hook and tell him the truth? *Why bother?* she argued with herself. Wasn't she already in too deep? She gave herself a few more weeks with Nate just to feel things out.

"Perhaps you shouldn't drive," he suggested.

"Not drive?" Amelia pulled away; her brows drew together in confusion. "I live right around the corner. What's up?"

"Sorry," Nate said. His flashy smile changed the somber mood between them. "I am not used to asking a pretty lady out on a date."

"Date?" Amelia's brows drew together again. If she didn't stop frowning, she might end up with a permanent wrinkle between her eyebrows. "We're beyond dating."

"In your book." Nate stepped closer. He enclosed her with his arms pressed against the hood of her door.

Excitement coursed through Amelia's veins. She licked her lips and glanced up at him. The sun caught his emerald green eyes. "Lord Jesus."

The boys on skateboards skated by with catcalls and whistles. Amelia hid her face in Nate's shoulder. He smelled of fresh soap. The neatly trimmed goatee lay against the smooth, honey-hued jawline.

"Seriously, though," Nate said, pressing a kiss against her temple, "what do you have planned today?"

"Nothing but running errands for Grandmamma. What about you?"

"Running errands for the girls." Nate laced his fingers with hers. Their fingers fit perfectly, just as everything else between them did. "Let's do them together."

"Errands together, huh?" Why did the idea excite her so much?

"Woman, you haven't experienced an afternoon of errands with me until we've tasted all the samples at kiosk stands at the grocery store, tried out all the exercise and massage displays."

And who would have guessed such domestication would have sounded so exciting?

A morning spent running errands had never been more romantic. After he followed her home to drop off the ice and say good morning to Mrs. Marlow, Nate and Amelia took off for the rest of the day. In the evening, he dropped her back to her grandmother's house and held hands with her once again as Amelia walked him to the front door. The sun had already set over the peach trees lining the edge of the Marlows' lawn.

"May I see you again tomorrow?" Nate asked politely. Whether she said yes or no didn't matter. He'd enjoyed himself so much today he decided they were going to spend every day together until they left for Villa San Juan— something he still needed to sell her on.

"Aren't you so formal?" asked Amelia, cocking her head to one side.

Nate leaned forward. "Well, you never know when your grandmother might be at the window watching."

Under the early moon's light, Amelia's cheeks reddened. "Don't remind me."

"I'll try but it's going to be hard."

"No pun intended, I bet."

Glancing down at his basketball shorts, Nate could not hide the desire rising in him. What was it about Amelia that had him as immature as the skateboarders outside the Piggly Wiggly this morning? "I meant hard in the sense of I'm not sure how long I can go without being able to touch you."

Amelia held their hands up in the air. "We're touching now."

"You know what I'm talking about." In case she wasn't sure, Nate leaned forward and planted a kiss against her juicy lips. She still tasted like the apple-pie ice cream she'd taught Kimber and Philly to make after school. Amelia let go of his hand and ran her fingers along his stomach and up toward his chest, where his heart beat fast from her mere touch. Nate captured her hand with his and pulled it down toward their sides and broke the kiss.

"We have next weekend."

"What weekend?"

"Labor Day." Nate copied her earlier move and cocked his head to the side. "Remember, my family has a little gathering. I saw the magazines you picked up today. Maybe getting out of town will take your mind off your old life."

Amelia chewed on her bottom lip and looked away for a moment before she squinted her eyes as if she remembered something. "I thought you told me you wore a tux to this thing."

"You're imagining me in one right now, aren't you?"

"I'm trying to imagine how you interpret tuxedo into a little gathering." Amelia poked the center of his chest.

"So you'll come?"

Before she got the chance to answer, a clanging sound pierced the early night. A dog howled somewhere in the distance and a flock of black birds flew away from the treetops behind Amelia's house. The two of them gave each other a slow glance. Nate motioned with his finger toward his lips, then motioned for her to stand still. He stepped off the bottom step and stalked down the ramp to the screened-in breezeway connecting the barn and the house. The bathroom window he'd jumped out from the other night was left open. Broken branches lay limp in the gardenia bush. An evening gust of wind whipped through the yard, knocking a tin pot over, revealing the culprit— a small dog had torn through a hole in the screen. In the darkness, Nate could not tell the breed but judging from the bark he had nothing to fear.

"Puffy," Amelia exclaimed, coming up behind Nate. Apparently Pastor Rivers had been holding on to the dog since her grandmother's accident.

He turned, lips pursed, sure he'd told her to stay back. "Puffy?" he asked dryly.

The fluffy dog leaped into Amelia's arms. "Don't blame me. My grandmamma has a thing for Sean Combs."

Nate shook his head, not sure he'd ever be surprised by this family. A light came and went off as quickly as it came on. "Your grandmother's home?"

"She should be." Amelia's brows rose.

"Stay here, and I mean it this time."

Amelia saluted with a half smile. Her sarcasm turned him on. He'd deal with her later but for now he wanted to make sure everything was okay in the Marlow household. Nate entered the breezeway through the screened-in porch and then into the back hall by the kitchen. Shuffling, like furniture moving around, came from Helen Marlow's new bedroom.

"I have a gun," Helen shouted.

"Mrs. Marlow, it's Nate Reyes."

"Who?"

Nate cleared his throat. He didn't recall Helen having memory problems. Maybe an extended nap in the quiet afternoon disorientated her. "Nate. I'm a friend of Amelia's."

"Parker?"

The reminder of Amelia's former beau was unnecessary. Nate cleared his throat deeper. "No, ma'am. It's Nate Reyes, I've brought Amelia home. Hang on a sec." Nate moved away from the door back into the kitchen and knocked on the window to motion at Amelia to come inside. In a matter of seconds Amelia appeared in the doorway, scruffy dog in hand.

"What's wrong?" she asked.

"Tell your grandmother who I am."

Brows drawn together, Amelia sighed and walked down the hall to her grandmother's door. "Grandmamma, open up."

"What do you want?" Helen barked instead of really asking.

"Grandmamma, why do you have the door locked?"

"Because you got strange men in my house at all times of the night," said Helen, opening her door just a crack.

Something about this situation seemed familiar. Nate tugged the hairs of his goatee and grinned, remembering his first night with Amelia and her former boss. The humor rising from his gut ceased at the memory. Today, they'd spent time touring the town. He wanted to be the one to take her around and show her all the changes and entice her into staying.

Amelia huffed, blowing a lock of her hair out of her eyes, and pushed away from Helen's door, taking Nate's hand in hers. Nate wanted more than anything to take her upstairs into her bedroom, but he stood still.

Amelia glanced upward. "Everything okay?"

The moonlight spilling in from the kitchen window framed her face with a halo. Nate pulled his hands from hers to cup her face. "Everything will be perfect if you agree to go away with me next weekend."

"What?" Amelia's voice echoed through the halls. "You're serious, aren't you?"

"As ever."

"Will Natalia be there?"

Nate shrugged his shoulders, knowing good and well she might. "I don't know."

"Will the folks from the school shooting be there?"

"Some of them," answered Nate, pressing his lips as he thought of his cousin in Orlando. Marisol Torres refused to ever step foot on the island again.

"What do you think of me doing a human interest story?" Amelia pressed on.

"Absolutely not."

Amelia's lips twisted to the left. "Well, who's going to be there?"

"Um," Nate hummed and pressed his lips against Amelia's. "Me?"

"Can I think about it?"

Trying to contain his disappointment, Nate smiled and brushed his thumb across her bottom lip. "I suppose that's better than a no. May I see you tomorrow?"

"Sorry." Amelia shook her head back and forth. "I've got to go over some footage with Lexi tomorrow and then we're heading down to Tallahassee to scout out some clients."

Nate's heart raced with excitement. He bit the inside of his cheek to contain himself. "Well, all right then." He sighed, feigning disappointment. "Let me know when the two of you return. Maybe we can get together for dinner."

"Maybe," Amelia said, taking his hands and walking him to the door.

"Still better than a no." Nate kissed her once more before exiting the Marlow household and jumping down the porch stairs. His plan of getting Amelia to stay was working.

Chapter 11

"I'm so embarrassed for you." Kimber Reyes gave a droll eye roll at her uncle before covering her face with embarrassment after Nate flipped a burger and gave a spin in front of the brick grill by the pool in the backyard of the Reyes home. A bright orange flame hissed out of the iron grates.

Glad she'd decided to come today, Amelia hid her giggle behind a feigned cough into the crook of her arm at the interaction between uncle and niece. Her arms smelled like a combination of strawberries and peaches from the gallons of ice cream she'd made up this morning and had chilling in the deep freezer.

"Traitor," said Nate over his shoulder where Amelia stretched out on a lawn chair.

Since the Reyeses weren't going to be in town next week for the three-day weekend, the uncles had decided to throw a pool party for Kimber and Philly's friends and neighbors for a pre-Labor Day celebration. Nate and Stephen had opened up the two-story split-level brick home that once belonged to their brother, Ken, and his wife. Amelia remembered Betty Gravel-Reyes with great fondness. Betty would have been proud of the lengths Nate and Stephen Reyes were going to to raise the girls.

It was also nice to see Jeanette and Enzo Gravel firmly established in their granddaughters' lives. Amelia understood why they had not contested Ken and Betty's will. But age did not stop them from being involved. Currently, the grandparents were blowing bubbles into the air over the pool while Philly and her friends jumped into the clear blue water to catch them.

Red, white and blue pinwheels surrounding the lagoon-style pool spun with the warm wind. The smaller children found the whimsical toys interesting and pulled some up out of the remarkably green grass to have a blowing contest. Kimber took a few minutes out of her time from entertaining a few girls and boys from her school to come and talk to Amelia.

Not having grown up with younger kids around her, Amelia found the hazel-eyed girl amusing. But she understood how the teenager would be embarrassed by things Nate or Stephen did. She remembered how humiliating it had been for herself when her father would moonwalk around on the floor of The Scoop as if he were Michael Jackson. To make things worse, their ice-cream parlor had been the local hangout of teenagers for the majority of her life here in Southwood. Amelia did not mind the little spin Nate did in his apron and bare chest. He wore a pair of green swim trunks which hung slightly off his waist and to his knees. When he took the apron off, Amelia found herself dumbfounded at the sight of the V-formation of his abs.

"Not a traitor, more like a sympathizer," Amelia explained with a stutter. Nate had that kind of effect on her whenever he flashed a grin. With his backyard barbecue and Southern hospitality, he certainly made a life in South-wood foreseeable. "I understand Kimber's pain."

"See," Kimber said. She beamed and poked her tongue out at her uncle. "You're being a pain."

Amelia chuckled and decided not to correct the girl. She commiserated with her pain, but as a woman she enjoyed watching Nate's muscles glisten with sweat under the blaring sun. Not like she'd tell him, though. Nate could use a bit of humility. Among the guests at the party were a lot of the mothers from Philly's pageant class. They had no shame when it came to the revealing bathing suits they wore or how high their heels were at a pool party. She'd heard the old saying, "The higher the heel, the closer to heaven," and these ladies truly needed Jesus. One mother of a younger boy bent over blatantly, straight-legged, in front of the grill to "admire" the pink perennials as she showed off *her* flower.

Territoriality was not a thing Amelia experienced often unless it came to her assignments. She loathed the idea of a man like William Vickers getting her prized executive producer position. In the early stages of her career as an assistant to the executive producers, she was paid hand-somely to egg on jealousy between some of the house-guests in her reality shows. She'd point out the attention one girl received from a lusted-after man or even how one girl copied another's dress style. But she herself experiencing possessiveness over a man? The notion was crazy... Although if someone gave her a dollar for each heavy sigh and eye roll she gave today, she'd be a millionaire before Nate and Stephen served lunch.

Karma was biting her in the ass with a heap load of in-securities, as well. Hell, she followed glamorous women around all the time, and she'd never felt the intensity of self-doubt as she did today. She sat here wearing a red halter-top, one-piece suit feeling like a plump tomato while these women who'd given birth sported svelte figures. She didn't expect Nate to have been a saint prior to meeting her, but she did wonder which of these women made up his days-of-the-week girls.

"Miss Amelia," began Kimber, "is it true you've worked with music producers?"

What Amelia had learned about Kimber was the girl loved the world of celebrities. "I have. Are you interested in meeting one?"

"I do love to sing."

A long list of singing competitions came to mind. Kimber would make the perfect contestant on any of the shows. She was young and gorgeous with a heart-tugging backstory. America would fall in love with her.

"I know that look." Cay interrupted Amelia's thoughts. "You've got a pitch going on in your head."

"A pitch?" uncle and niece chorused.

"My cousin has this knack of turning everything she comes across into a reality show," Cay continued, ignoring Amelia's death stare that was willing her to shut up. The cousins had met up at Grandmamma's to prepare the ice-cream treats for this afternoon. They'd rummaged through the barn for novelty items such as the old-fashioned red-and-white ice-cream stand equipped with a red-and-white striped tarp, under which the kids loved hanging out in the shade while poring over the wide variety of treats. Along with the standard flavors of ice cream like chocolate and vanilla, they'd also made peach, strawberry and even bubblegum ice cream. Though Amelia informed Cay that she still hadn't told Nate the truth about her employment status, she did not want this barbecue to be the place for the discussion.

"Yeah, I recognize that look." Nate studied Amelia's face and shook his head back and forth. "Too bad there will be no reality shows here, not in this household." Nate frowned.

A twinge of hurt tugged at Amelia's heart. Her bottom lip poked out. "You haven't even heard my pitch."

"It doesn't matter," said Nate, turning his back to the burgers and hot dogs. "My niece won't be involved."

"Don't be mean, Uncle Nate."

"Who?"

Kimber sighed in annoyance. "*Tío* Nate. And don't change the subject. Let's listen to what Miss Amelia has to say about my singing career."

"Miss Amelia," Nate clipped, "doesn't have a say in your nonexistent singing career."

The fun, sun-loving, pool-splashing atmosphere continued as Amelia swallowed her feelings. The pangs stemming from her heart vibrated through her body. Nate's icy tone reminded her of the scolding and sometimes cursing out she received from contestants after she purposely manipulated a situation just to get a money shot. Over the years, she'd done some shady things, but producing reality shows was her life. And from the tone in his voice she could tell he despised her lifestyle. Had his back not been turned, she probably would have seen his upper lip curled.

"Don't pay him any attention," said Kimber, patting Amelia's hand. The girl's bright smile cheered her up a bit. "He doesn't know good television. Let's talk about Natalia. Do you know where she is?"

"Unfortunately, I don't," Amelia answered, though she wondered if the star of the show was hiding in retaliation. "I'm starting to get worried."

"Well, if you ask me, I think Natalia is tired of living her life in front of the camera." Kimber's perception gave Amelia reason to pause.

"You think?"

Kimber shrugged her shoulders. "She didn't seem happy."

"What?"

"Every time the camera caught her in the background of her brother Nicholas or her sister Natasha, she got this far-off kind of look. Natasha's preparing for a wedding and Nicholas is always dating. Maybe Natalia wants to settle down."

Hmm, Natalia settling down? A *Bachelorette* type of show? The ideas flew into her mind.

Dear MET executives,
With the Ruiz family climbing the reality TV charts,
I would like to schedule a pitch session to discuss
The Road to Ruiz Love.
Sincerely,
Amelia

"Is that the look when she's got an idea?" Kimber half whispered to Cay.

"Yep, that's it all right."

Amelia blinked back in focus in time to catch Nate shaking his head in disapproval. What did she need his approval for? This was her career she was thinking about. Backyard barbecues were one thing, but were they the rest of her life? Amelia sighed inwardly. She had a lot of thinking to do over the next few days.

"I have the perfect dress for you."

Amelia glanced up at the video footage she'd been editing all day long. The only time she recalled moving from the computer was to put on her favorite comfy, army-green hooded jacket from the coatrack by Lexi's office door. As she worked, whether she had multiple monitors to edit or one, Amelia had turned the lights off. When Lexi entered her office, the light from the main floor spilled through, blinding Amelia like a vampire. She ducked behind the monitor and clutched her heart.

"Sorry." Lexi cocked her head and grinned. She reached for the light switch with her long purple nails that matched her sparkly tutu. According to the chaotic whiteboard schedule, the afternoons were dedicated to a dance rehearsal led by Chantal Hairston, Lexi's right-hand woman for the pageant coaching. Amelia couldn't help observing the contrast in the way she and Lexi were dressed. While Lexi looked like a prima ballerina, here Amelia sat in her faded comfy jeans and an old red Southwood High T-shirt.

"I thought the bell over the door didn't ding when I came back into the store," Lexi continued, stepping farther into her office, but she turned to glance at the front door to the shop. "Damn it, I'm probably going to have to get a new bell. I can't have customers sneaking in on me. You never know what I might be doing with the hot new neighbor."

The hot new neighbor, as Amelia had learned last week, was none other than Stephen Reyes. He ran the new real estate and contracting agency in town. Over one of their dinners, Nate had shared with Amelia information about the business he and his brother owned. The brothers did a lot of scouting for television and movie execs—namely for MET—which probably explained Nate's ability to contact Natalia so easily. She hinted again for the real story, but he declined—as always. Each brother had their own niche in the business. Stephen worked more with the Hollywood folks in the aspect of helping people get into their dream homes. Most of the homes, as Amelia understood, were replicas of iconic houses from the movies. If the frame of the desired homes needed work, Nate stepped in to reconstruct the buildings. Amelia understood Nate's passion for tweaking the homes exactly how the home buyers wanted them to be. *The man was good with his hands.* Amelia rolled her eyes at her new friend and shook her head, not expecting the crick in her shoulders.

Three of the mandatory weeks were already up. When was the last time she'd woken up in the same bed for a full week? Two months ago, Amelia was jet-setting across the country. The mere thought of staying in one place for any amount of time seemed dull, and yet, these last few weeks had flown by.

Amelia had traveled to and from Grits and Glam Gowns in Grandmamma's car and never once complained about being stuck behind a tractor. She didn't bat an eye when someone parked their horse in a diagonal spot in front of the coffee shop on the corner. The road trips she took with Lexi and her Glam Squad never maxed more than two hours and the largest body of water they crossed was the Flint River.

This morning Amelia had arrived just after eight and judging from the clock in the right-hand corner of the monitor she used, the sun was about to set. Where was Nate? The last time she'd laid eyes on him, or hands, for that matter, he'd walked her to the front doors of Grits and Glam Gowns. He'd placed his hands on the rim of the door to stop himself from entering and defiling the gowns in his future sister-in-law's store. Maybe during their heated kiss, he'd knocked the bell off-kilter. Amelia adored Nate, but as these weeks flew by, so had the time they had to be intimate. Since Grandmamma's return from the hospital,

Nate had become the ultimate choir boy. Was it possible to miss someone—sexually—after a few times?

Cheeks flushed at the memory, Amelia fanned her face. "My goodness, I forgot how time flies when editing."

"So you think you can come up with something?" Lexi asked, strutting across the length of her office.

"Not just something," Amelia bragged, "some things."

"I hope this hasn't been too much trouble."

"Not at all." Amelia waved off the notion. "I've come up with the perfect video for you to give Emily and Sam." She beamed. "I also took the liberty of putting together footage for you to give your potential clients. I like the regular portfolio, but sometimes having a visual of what it looks like to win helps. I noticed you've built your clientele based on each pageant win and word of mouth. This way you'll have a portfolio potential pageant clients can see."

"Let me see." Lexi came over to Amelia's side of the desk and leaned over to view what Amelia had come up with.

Amelia waited, nervous at Lexi's response. The bubbles in the pit of her stomach were refreshing. When was the last time she'd gotten excited and nervous over her job? *Damn, she missed working.* Sure, the bubbles of excitement welled inside of her body when she thought of seeing Nate again, too; the two feelings were very similar. One, however, gave her orgasms.

"This is awesome, Amelia," exclaimed Lexi once the video ended. "I don't know how to thank you."

"You don't have to thank me." Amelia shook her head. "This is what I do for a living."

"*Did?* Right?" asked Lexi. "Nate shared with me he got you fired. I know I might not be able to pay much but I could really use your help around here."

"Lexi," Amelia started.

"No, I'm serious. Grits and Glam Gowns is more than just a dress shop. I've got weddings, proms and all other kinds of events needing a videographer."

Amelia needed to stop her. She shook her head and held up her hand. "Lexi, my job is not in jeopardy. I'm on mandatory leave."

"What?" Lexi stepped with a dramatic flair.

"I was never fired," Amelia confessed. She watched the news register through Lexi's wide eyes and immediately began to explain. "When everything happened with Nate, I did miss an opportunity for some great sound points on the show I produce. So my boss felt I might be overworked. With Grandmamma getting ill and me not taking a sick day in years, he ordered a mandatory leave of at least one month."

Lexi covered her mouth with her French-manicured hands. "You've been here for three weeks."

"I know."

"Because of Miss Helen?"

Amelia blinked and glanced toward the screen. "Would you judge me if I said Nate was a part of the reason?"

A pregnant pause of shame fell between them. Amelia thought of herself as a career woman, not someone who put her life on hold for a man. And the crazy thing about extending her time to be with Nate was that it was purely on an emotional level. If it were for the sex, she'd understand, but with each day passing she found herself growing more attached to Nate.

"Hey, don't be embarrassed. I fell in love with one of those Reyes boys," said Lexi. "I completely understand."

"No one said anything about love," Amelia said, panicking. "I've produced shows where people claim to fall in love with someone after one date, seen folks get married after laying eyes on each other for the first time. I've seen some pretty bizarre things out in the world."

"This is reality," Lexi said, patting Amelia's shoulder, "and realistic. You and Nate clearly have the chemistry. The two of you can't stop making goo-goo eyes at each other."

Amelia pressed her lips together to keep from grinning. "You've been talking to Philly."

"Give the girl something sweet and she'll spill all your secrets." Lexi chuckled and patted Amelia's shoulder again. "Look, girl, I'm not going to say anything to Nate about your job, but you need to. Sooner or later, you're going to have to make a decision."

"Why?"

"Because you can't be in a serious relationship if you're traveling all the time working on reality shows."

Amelia's lips twisted. Maybe she could manage her career as well as a relationship with Nate. Time would tell—and by time, she had until this weekend to decide.

Well aware of the silence falling between them since they'd left Lexi's shop that evening, Nate reached across the console of his SUV for Amelia's hand.

"Everything okay?"

The car passed under a street lamp. The light illuminated Amelia's face. Nate's heart seized for a brief moment when she smiled. He'd never get tired of it. "You're awfully quiet."

"Lexi made me a dress."

"She thinks you're special," said Nate. "Something wrong with her making you a dress?"

"It's for your small gathering Saturday night."

Nate bit down on the inside of his cheek to contain his

excitement. "Oh, yeah?" His mind raced with all the places he wanted to take her in his hometown.

"I haven't agreed to go."

"I fully believe you'll change your mind." Nate turned his vehicle onto the graveled driveway. The tires crunching against the tiny rocks reminded him of the next task he wanted to do for Amelia and Helen. Even though Helen was still in a cast, she'd eventually have a cane. A cane and gravel did not mix. "Want me to bring you in to work tomorrow after I drop off the girls at school?"

The norm for the last week had been for him to pick Amelia up and bring her into town to work with Lexi. He looked forward to their routine. Who knew a relationship would be fun? Why did everyone think it was hard work? The hardest thing, Nate might argue, was the sex, or lack of it. At their age, a quickie in the car was not an every-day thing—hence why he also wanted to get away for the weekend. The girls would stay with his parents and he'd get a room at the Torres Towers, his family's hotel.

"Sounds like a plan to me, unless you want to stay the night and be here already in the morning."

The lower extremities of his body thumped with lust. Nate swallowed down his desire. "Temptress."

"So you're telling me no?"

"I've got to get back to the house." Nate reached over and stroked her neck. "It's my turn to cook."

Amelia shrugged off his touch and reached for the silver handle. For a moment his feelings were hurt from the rejection until she flashed a smile. "Are the girls on punishment or something?"

"You got jokes?"

Before Amelia got a chance to come back with a smart-alecky remark, a flock of startled birds flew from behind the barn. The sun hadn't made its way over the treetops but the near moon hovered along the horizon. An animal larger than Helen's pet howled.

"Stay in the car," he ordered Amelia. "I mean it."

"And if there is a wolf or coyote behind the barn—" Amelia's eyes widened with fear "—what are you going to do? It might even be a bear."

"How often do bears come around here?" Nate jogged to the front of the car and then darted off to the trees to snag a branch. Satisfied with the weight, he stalked toward the screen door. Whatever made the noise was still back in the barn, not outside. Coyotes, wolves or bears could not open doors. Nate wedged himself through the screen door enough before the hinges squeaked and hiked the branch like a bat over his shoulder. Prepared to swing like Derek Jeter, Nate said a silent prayer bears hadn't learned how to open doors.

"Whoever's in there," he said, making his voice deeper, "I'm coming in swinging."

The light above the doors back into the house switched on. For a moment he thought the blinding beam came on as a motion detector, but Helen Marlow banged on the glass, her pinched face frowning.

"What the hell are you doing back at my house?" Helen snarled through the glass.

"Evening, Miss Helen." Nate brought the bat back down to his side. "I did not mean to startle you." He figured telling her an animal prowled somewhere in her backyard or possibly barn would only startle her further.

"You still did not answer me."

"Grandmamma," Amelia called out from the passenger's seat.

"I was bringing Amelia home, Miss Helen," said Nate.

The brass doorknob turned and the door opened. Helen

poked her head out. A blue cast wedged through the crack. "Why is she in the car?"

Nate cleared his throat, not sure how to answer—still not wanting to frighten her. "I wanted to make..."

"You wanted to get a peep at an old lady, didn't you?" Helen raised one brow and frowned before eventually breaking out a hacking cough as she laughed. "Boy, I'm just messing with you. Y'all stop playing around out here and get inside."

Relieved she wasn't upset, Nate set the makeshift bat down and signaled for Amelia to come on inside.

"You like my granddaughter, don't you?" Helen asked.

"Yes, ma'am, I do."

"Well, then, I don't understand what you two are doing here," Helen said under her breath. "I would have figured the two of you young folks would be rolling around in a bed somewhere." Choking on air, Nate began to cough. "Don't be shocked, darling, I was young once, too."

"Grandmamma," Amelia said, arriving at the screen door of the breezeway. "What are you doing out of bed?"

Helen Marlow cocked her hand on her hip and studied her granddaughter. "You'd like for this old woman to be bedridden, wouldn't you?"

Beside him, Amelia huffed out a sigh and rolled her eyes. "Of course not, Grandmamma. I want to make sure you're getting enough rest so your broken leg will heal properly so you don't have to go back to the hospital and disturb those nice people."

Matching her granddaughter's sigh and eye roll, Helen turned around and waltzed back into the house, leaving the two of them alone. Whatever might have been in the barn must have been scared off. The threats coming from both sides now were gone.

"Well, I better leave, as well," he said.

"Are you sure?" Amelia asked.

The soft batting of her lashes tempted him to stay. He wanted to see them flutter in the midst of a climax. But Nate held strong. "No, I'm not, but I am trying to do the right thing here."

"Which is?"

"Amelia." Nate sighed heavily and took her hand in his. "I would love more than anything in the world to stay here with you, but I have my nieces I need to look out for. I don't want them to get the wrong idea about us."

"Us, or you?" Amelia asked out of nowhere.

"What?"

Amelia shook her head and then smiled. "I'm sorry. I am a bit cranky. You head on back and I'll see you in the morning."

Just because Nate had a curfew didn't mean Amelia did. So when Chantal stopped by with the last cartridge of footage on her way to the club, Amelia took her up on the offer to come along. From what she'd learned, Chantal was talented as well as smart. She helped Lexi out at Grits and Glam Gowns, not only with the books but with the pageant choreography. Now that Chantal had recently graduated with her MBA, she actually was able to get paid as a bookkeeper-slash-dancer.

"It's not the dancing my grandmother wants to brag about," Chantal said, circling the rim of her wineglass with her index finger. They sat in the VIP section, watching the patrons on the dance floor below.

"Don't get me started on grandmothers." She liked the young dancer a lot; they had a lot in common. Both women worked hard and spent a lot of time on their phones. Tonight, however, proved to be a difference between the two of them; Amelia had forgotten her cell phone at home.

"That's right." Chantal laughed. "At least we don't have to see our families all the time."

Moisture began to pool at the stem of Amelia's glass. After Nate left, she and Grandmamma had discussed different flavor ideas for ice cream. Having the old equipment dragged out onto the breezeway had gotten Grandmamma all nostalgic. She even wanted to send Amelia out to the store to pick up the ingredients, but when Chantal came over, Grandmamma had ushered her out the door. Things were certainly different now that she was older. Grandmamma was slightly easier to get along with. Would staying here be so bad?

"Well," Amelia said with a sigh, not knowing what to say. Was she seriously thinking about staying here?

A slow smile spread across Chantal's face. "Do I hear hesitation in that 'well'?"

Heat reached Amelia's cheeks before she could register her embarrassment. "I'm not saying Southwood is all bad. And after last week's barbecue, my cousin Cay has been set on reopening the family's ice-cream parlor."

"You better snatch up the property soon," said Chantal. "A lot of developers have been vying for that location."

"I know. I can't believe it hasn't been bought yet." When her parents had closed up shop, they had done so leaving a lot of things intact—the original flooring, the wall-unit freezer, even the cases for the bins of ice cream. Cay's idea to reopen the place had really stuck with Amelia. Cay didn't have the equity for the place, but Amelia did. Working with her cousin had been fun. And who knew? With the flavors they came up with, the foodies visiting Southwood would literally eat it up.

Amelia didn't mind the revamping of the city or the traffic it brought in. If travelers wanted to spend time in an authentic small town, who was she to point fingers?

As a matter of fact, it might make for an interesting pitch to MET. *Small town, big bucks?*

"It helps having a hot guy like Nate to persuade you, huh?"

"Nate helps," said Amelia. "It's nice knowing not everyone hates me."

"I can't imagine anyone hating you."

At that inopportune moment Brittany Foley entered the VIP section, stumbling over her four-inch heels at the top step. Their eyes locked and Amelia resisted the urge to smirk when Brittany's lip rose in a snarl. "No need to imagine, here's one right now."

Chantal scoffed at the comment. "Brittany doesn't count. You're occupying her man."

My man, Amelia thought.

"I mean, the man she thinks is hers," Chantal corrected herself. "Now, with you here, he's off the market. If you leave, there might just be a feeding frenzy."

If, the one little word that struck a chord with Amelia. "Nate is a big boy. He can handle himself."

"Of course Nate is a big boy," Brittany snarled as she approached. "And now that you're not forcing him to be with you…"

"Oh, come on now, Brittany," Chantal cooed. "She can't be forcing him too much if Nate is the one begging her to go home with him this weekend."

As a field producer for catty reality shows, Amelia earned cash bonuses for money shots. The opened mouth, stretched face and rush of red across Brittany's cheeks would have gotten Amelia the bonus of a lifetime. Staying in town just to keep the look of shock on Brittany's face might be worth it.

"You know what," Brittany began, her eyes crinkled at the corners of her eyes. "Y'all need Jesus. I'm going to pray for you, something which I can do because my grandfather, Pastor Rivers, taught me to do that for my enemies."

"Whatever you say," Amelia sneered.

"What I say," Brittany gritted, "is you ought to be careful who you're messing with. Karma is a bitch when you mess with God's children."

After Brittany walked through the VIP section, Amelia and Chantal broke out in a fit of laughter. One thing Amelia didn't miss about being back home was the hypocrites. She shook her head to push Brittany and her attempt at preaching out of her mind, and then realized what she'd said. A warm feeling of relaxation washed over her. *She was back home.*

Amelia couldn't wait to get home and call Nate. When Chantal received a text from a potential client, Amelia didn't hesitate to say yes and hop in the car. Instead of making her drive up the gravel way and risk waking Grandmamma, Amelia stepped out of the car, kicked out of her heels and hightailed it through the green grass, up the ramp and ran inside. The screams she made should have woken the closest neighbors down the road. The last thing she expected to see in her grandmother's living room was her grandmamma sprawled out on the living room floor, with Pastor Rivers scrambling to cover his naked body.

Chapter 12

Nate cared less about what had made Amelia change her mind so quickly and more about the reality of her being in his hometown with him. Their five-hour drive was filled with nonstop chatter from both equally excited girls. Not even a chauffeured ride from Stephen's driver, Keenan, diverted the girls' desire to hang out with Amelia. Nate liked the idea of the girls liking Amelia. If they didn't get along, a relationship between him and Amelia might have to be readjusted. But considering the way Amelia offered advice and listened to the girls, she cared as well about them. Nate wasn't particularly happy about Kimber's eagerness to bend Amelia's ear about getting into the reality TV world, but he was sure he'd nipped the idea in the bud during the barbecue. According to the feedback he'd received from Chantal last night, Amelia seemed more and more driven to want to stay in Southwood—just as he planned.

Why would she need the flashy lights from all the cameras or all the action and drama from her previous life? When they stopped off at his mother's house, Nate quickly regretted his decision to bring her because his mother's infatuation with Amelia only excited Amelia, as well. She beamed from ear to ear, telling his mother about the trips she'd taken with the Ruiz clan back to Puerto Rico. Amelia's oval face lit up with animated excitement when his mother mentioned restaurants and places she'd visited. He'd worked so hard these past few weeks getting Amelia to start her new life over in Southwood instead of trying to get her old job back or even continue in the television industry. What she needed to see was that settling down back home was the right choice for her. And him.

Now, finally alone with no responsibility other than to attend to her every wish and command, Nate breathed a sigh of relief after he stepped out of the shower and spotted Amelia. She stood against the balcony of their Torres Towers Hotel suite with the sun settling down into the Gulf as a backdrop behind her. The white sequined dress sparkled under the pink sky. Her long, shapely legs beckoned to be wrapped around his waist. A sea breeze filtered through the air, lifting Amelia's shoulder-length hair off her neck, exposing a ripe place to plant a kiss right along her collarbone. Having kept her body at bay, he felt the sexual desire in him grow stronger knowing they had the whole weekend together. The breeze made its way into the living room of the suite and offered a teasing hint of Amelia's sweet, peachy scent. Mouth watering, Nate licked his lips and cleared his throat. At the sound, their eyes locked. A familiar beat thumped against Nate's rib cage. He pressed his hand against the pocket of his white Oxford shirt to make sure his heart did not beat out his chest. The last time this happened was the night he'd first made eye contact with Amelia. At the time, he'd thought he would only buy her a drink to keep her occupied. but now he wanted so much more. He needed her, now.

Tonight he'd made a reservation at Ignacio's, the salsa dinner club off the boardwalk. He'd missed the spiciness of the food and the action on the dance floor. But given that his uncle Ignacio owned the place, he trusted his table would still be held for them.

"Did you say something?" Amelia asked.

"I may have, but whatever words I had got stuck in my throat when I saw you." At this point Nate found no reason to hold his feelings back. She'd infiltrated his life and his heart. "I love you, Amelia."

Whether or not it was the pink sky or her feelings, a blush crept across her high cheekbones. Given what he'd learned of her job, he wished he'd had a camera to capture this tender moment. Amelia needed a close-up shot of her face. Never one for a loss of words, she stood there, dumbfounded.

"Too soon?" he asked. For a moment he wondered if he'd scared her off. Hell, the words scared him. Nate had never been in this position before. But all he could think about was her. The only person he wanted to be with was Amelia.

A single tear glistened in the corner of her left eye. "You love me?"

"I do."

"Nate, I—"

Nate closed the distance between them, gently wrapping his fingers around her slender neck to bring her face closer to his. They both paused for a quick breath before desire consumed him. Every inch of his body hardened. Afraid he'd burst if he didn't hold her, Nate swept her into his arms and carried her through the living room area, kitchen, down the hall and to their bedroom. The backs of her soft thighs pressed against his forearms. Her heartbeat raced through her clothing against his chest. He'd won her over, he felt it, but knew she didn't know how to express it. In a moment, she could show him. Nate kicked the bedroom door open.

"Hey now," Amelia gasped. "I thought we had reservations."

"They can wait," he replied, trailing a set of kisses along her neck. She tasted as sweet as she smelled. "I can't."

Nate set Amelia down on the bed facing him. Leaning forward, he kissed her and coaxed her to stretch out on the bed. Nate extended his body over hers, balancing himself on his knees at the edge of the king-size mattress. With one hand holding his upper body above her head, he used the other to span across her body, aiming toward the hem of her dress. To his surprise, she wore only that tonight.

"Naughty, naughty," he whispered in her ear.

"I already knew you wouldn't be able to resist me." Amelia's lips spread into a grin against his earlobe.

"You set me up?" Nate's blood pulsed when her teeth nibbled his ear.

"More like, I came prepared." With her challenging tone, Amelia wrapped her legs around his waist and drew him close against the nectar between her legs.

The heat sizzled against his growing erection. Damn his pants. Caught up in sensation, Nate lost focus and Amelia took over. Her legs squeezed and maneuvered so he was somehow lying flat on the mattress. As he did with her, Amelia assumed his previous position, one hand by his head supporting her weight and the other slowly traveling down toward the waistband of his black slacks.

"Nathaniel." Infamous chef Ignacio Torres made his way toward the white-clothed, two-top intimate table overlooking the jam-packed dance floor. He'd just finished doing a number with a few pretty customers before he spied his nephew. Prior to being seated, Nate explained that his uncle enjoyed pulling ladies out of their seats and dancing with them. He said people lined up praying to get chosen by the dancing chef.

Celebrities were a part of Amelia's career. She filmed them, followed them and recruited them for guest appearances. Being starstruck was not something she usually went through, but when charismatic Ignacio danced his way up the winding glass stairway toward them she beamed from ear to ear. For a moment she debated whether or not to reach for a napkin and ask for an autograph. Instead, she accepted the hug Nate's uncle gave her, feeling it to be more valuable than a signature. He accepted her immediately.

"It is an honor to have you at my establishment, Miss Marlow." Ignacio spoke in a thick Puerto Rican accent.

A menagerie of scents stemming from onions, bell peppers, cilantro and *culantro*, which made up a batch of *sofrito* and *recaito*, whetted Amelia's appetite. She and Nate had certainly worked up one before arriving tonight. Coming to his feet, Nate broke up the two-second-too-long hung from Ignacio and clasped his uncle on the back for a half hug.

"All right, all right," said Nate. "Hands off my woman."

Ignacio cut a look over at Amelia and winked. "I knew you were special the moment Nate said he wanted a table for two."

Heart fluttering when Nate turned his gaze away for a brief moment, Amelia smiled. "For real?"

"I would not lie," said Ignacio, crossing his heart with his index finger. "And I can honestly say I understand why he wants you all to himself. You are absolutely beautiful."

Nate cleared his throat. "Need I remind you she's my date?"

"Two handsome men fighting over me?" Amelia inhaled deeply.

Dear MET executives,
Sizzle with salsa on this small island town with the
Torres family, where the men all have the same taste
in beautiful women. I would like to schedule a pitch
session to discuss Keeping it in the Family.
Sincerely,
Amelia

"Uh-oh." Nate waved his hand in front of Amelia's face. "*Tío,* we need to hurry up and get some food in her."

Ignacio nodded and excused himself, backing away from the table with the promise of such fine cuisine that she'd go home with him instead of Nate. After Nate seated Amelia, she watched him sit back down, smoothing the front of his blue shirt. The white one he'd worn before lay tattered on the floor in their bedroom, courtesy of her. And she didn't feel the slightest bit of guilt for doing so. Being able to make love to Nate wherever and whenever was liberating.

"Don't think I didn't catch the faraway look in your eyes," Nate said; a twinkle sparked in his green eyes.

Amelia batted her lashes over the single candle between them. A soft trumpet solo played on the stage below. "What?"

"C'mon, tell me what the idea for a reality show was."

"The only thing I am willing to share is that it was about family." It was mostly the truth.

Nate rested his elbows on the table. "You miss your old job, don't you?"

Since telling him the little white lie about losing her job, Amelia never had found the right time to confess. Besides, anytime someone brought up her career, Nate found a way to change the subject. Just the other day he shut down any conversation Kimber wanted to have over the whole reality show topic.

"I worked really hard to get where I was, Nate," Amelia answered with a thoughtful sigh. It was the truth.

Climbing the ladder had been her priority before she was placed on leave. Now, not so much. It had been what she wanted to share with Nate last night before walking in on her grandmother and Pastor Rivers's lovemaking session. The thought caused her to cringe. Eyes closed tight, Amelia shook her head. When she opened them, Nate was sitting back in his chair with a brow raised. The corners of his full lips were turned upward in an amused grin. Wanton desire electrified her system. She had to look away. If she didn't, she was sure she'd climb across the table and into his lap.

In order to keep her clothes from coming off so fast in front of these strangers, Amelia turned her attention to the patrons of the restaurant. Even though she'd resolved her feelings about Southwood, something on the dance floor caught her attention, or at least someone did. Amelia shook her head and blinked. Natalia Ruiz. The familiar figure was cuddled close to a large person and had turned her face into his chest. Perhaps Amelia was seeing things. Her desire for Nate meant more than her desire to break up the dancing lovers' embrace just to satisfy her curiosity.

"Are you all right?"

Nate's deep voice brought her out of her daze. "I'm fine." She turned her attention back to her handsome date.

"I'm glad you're here," he said.

"I'm glad I'm here, too," Amelia said. "I can't believe I

have never been to Villa San Juan before. I can't wait for you to show me around."

"After dinner, we can take a walk down to the pier. Do you like history?"

"Love it."

"Great, there's an old bench we can hang out at and talk."

Amelia's brows rose. "A bench?"

"It has sentimental value. Lots of people propose there."

Amelia's brows froze in position. "What?"

Nate shook his head. "Whoa, I'm not proposing."

His quick response hurt her feelings. Though a part of Amelia knew marriage was not in her near future, did he have to respond with such disgust? Amelia faked a smile and inhaled. What was the point of her staying in Southwood if there was no future with Nate? Sure, there was more to staying in Southwood than a man. She'd reconnected with her family and the idea of reopening the ice-cream parlor was beginning to take shape. Her future was not based on a man, but still, Amelia decided to keep the truth about her job to herself.

"You're quiet now," noted Nate.

Amelia exhaled. "I'm fine."

Whether or not he believed her, Nate nodded and carried on the conversation, giving her a history lesson about his island. Another family member came over and said hello. Nate made his introductions and then asked if she minded if he stepped outside with him for a moment. Needing a break from him, Amelia offered a smile of permission. With Nate away, her eyes wandered toward the dance floor to where she thought she'd spotted Natalia. The dark hair and the height looked to be the same. Curious, Amelia pushed her chair away from the table. She had to get a better look.

Careful not trip on the silver four-inch silver heels Lexi insisted would "make the outfit," Amelia made her way down the crystal staircase through the crowds of salsa dancers. The couple she thought she'd seen had disappeared. Amelia stood in the center of the dance floor feeling foolish as hell. What would she have done if she spotted Natalia? Called who? Rory? Her film crew? William Vickers? Amelia shuddered at the thought.

What did any of it matter? She wanted to stay in Southwood. She'd already transferred the money to Cay's account. She'd chosen Southwood. She'd chosen the opportunity to be with Nate, even if he wasn't sure about their future. Amelia started to turn on her heels to head back to the table. Out of the corner of her eye she thought she spotted another familiar face, the runaway bride from the Ramos-Montenegro wedding earlier this summer. Grace, was it? Jesus, of all the times to not have her work phone! More importantly, of all the times to consider stepping down from her position at MET. If that was really Grace Montenegro or if that really had been Natalia, Amelia stood the chance to score TV gold.

"You didn't want to wait for me to dance?"

Heart racing, Amelia glanced upward. Butterflies floated against her rib cage at the sight of Nate standing in front of her. The tempo of a rumba pounded through the dance floor. Nate pulled her up against his body and, as usual, swept her off her feet. All doubts left when she was in his arms.

The following evening's main event for the weekend centered on the Crystal Coquí Ball. Several members of the Reyes-Torres families arrived in the ballroom. Men were dressed in tuxedos and women in their finest gowns. For once Amelia did not feel like a sore thumb sticking out among gorgeous people. Lexi and her glam squad had bombarded and taken over the hotel room, fortunately a few minutes after Nate and Amelia had finished another round of lovemaking. Two hours after the first knock on the door, Amelia stepped out into the living room in a formfitting peach gown. The shape of the halter top gave her cleavage for days. Judging from the way Nate's jaw dropped, she looked good.

A Caribbean band played in the background as guests arrived. A group of paparazzi hounded the patrons from the entrance. Amelia wished she had a camera just to capture all the beauty. Tonight's event was a Caribbean Done Good evening, celebrating the history makers. Classic art hung from the walls with spotlights perched underneath. Wineglasses clinked, and the smell of delicious food floated through the air.

"Are you glad you came?"

Amelia smiled up and over at her dinner date. The tuxedo fit Nate like a glove. His close-cropped hair reminded her of their first night together. His green eyes lit up when he smiled. Tonight he was her personal James Bond. "I'm honored to be here."

"This can't be better than being at a TV premiere," Kimber said, leaning forward. She sat at the same table with them, dressed in a royal blue, kid-length strapless gown.

Nate cut his eyes at his niece. "We're not going to make Amelia think about her old job."

"There is no old job."

The voice came from behind Amelia and Nate's chair. The two of them spun around. The moment Amelia spied the intruder. "Brittany."

Amelia didn't realize she and Nate had spoken at the same time until Nate continued speaking. "Why are you still here?"

Still here? Why was she even here in the first place?

"Nate, what's going on?" Nate's mother asked.

"Nada." Nate stood up from the table. "Brittany, may I speak to you in private?"

A few people from the nearby tables began to watch the interaction. In her previous job this TV gold moment would have made her signal for two cameras, one on Nate's narrowing eyebrows and Brittany's faux innocent, blinking lashes. This awkward moment was about to bring embarrassment to these people who'd been nothing but nice to her. Nate whisked Brittany off. By no means did Amelia plan on letting them speak together. She teetered in her heels down the private hallway and passed smiles to the guests. The woman seated at the table filled with older people was no doubt Grace Montenegro. In an attempt to get another visual on the runaway bride, Amelia bounced squarely into another figure. An apology flew out of her mouth before she recognized the face.

"Amelia?"

"Natalia?"

Without all the extra makeup, eyelashes and makeup, Natalia looked like a regular person. She wore her hair in a side bun, with no extra extensions. Mascara edged her lashes but did not overpower her eyes. With Amelia in stilettos and Natalia in flats, they were the same height. Both recognizing the drastic changes in each other, the women embraced each other.

"Where have you been?" Amelia asked.

"If you weren't going to be my producer, I wasn't going to film."

As expected, Natalia had no idea just how her actions affected everyone. "You're crazy, you know that?"

"Sure I am," said Natalia, "and what does that make

you? And who are you here with? Did I see Nate Reyes? Are you two here together?"

"One question at a time," Amelia said, laughing. "Who are you here with?"

Natalia glanced around Amelia's frame. "Are you wearing a mic?"

"No."

"So no production crew?"

Amelia shook her head left and right. "I'm taking more time."

"Is your grandmother okay?" Natalia's hands flew to her mouth. No polish, no jewels, just a low-key Natalia.

"Yes," Amelia said with a nod, "she's better than fine. I am actually here with Nate."

"Girl," Natalia hummed.

"Do you want to tell me who you're with? I thought I saw you last night dancing with some guy."

Natalia shook her head back and forth. "No, not just yet. He's special and kind of shy."

"If I didn't know any better, I'd say you were in love." Amelia cocked her head to the side when Natalia did not deny it. "Natalia!"

"I don't want to jinx anything," Natalia whined. "Please don't say anything to anyone yet."

If Amelia wanted her job and a promotion, she could leak this information. But what she wanted most right now was a moment alone with Nate. "We're friends, Natalia," Amelia assured her. "I promise I won't say anything."

Natalia threw her arms around Amelia's neck and squealed. "Thank you. Now you go find your man."

Taking her friend's advice, Amelia headed off toward the balcony where she last saw Nate's head. Outside, the ocean air filled her lungs. She spotted Nate's tall frame against the brick railing. His arms were folded across his chest. Brittany made eye contact with Amelia. Her devilish smirk sent chills down Amelia's spine.

"Here she is now," Brittany said. "Ask her yourself."

"Ask me what?" Amelia stepped over them and sidled up next to Nate. Instinctively he wrapped his arm around her shoulders. The summer night was anything but cold, yet Nate's touch still warmed her.

Instead of answering her, Brittany held out her phone and pressed a button. A distant conversation began. Amelia closed one eye and tried to pick up the familiarity of the voices. It was a conversation she had with Lexi about her not being fired. How in the hell did she record that? Then she remembered that the bell over the door at Grits and Glam Gowns was broken. Brittany could have walked in at any moment. When Amelia's confession ended on the recorder, Brittany clicked the stop button and smirked.

"See," Brittany said, beaming. "I told you I had proof she has been playing you."

"And I told you last night that I didn't care what you had on Amelia," Nate gritted out. "I am with her."

"You'd take this heathen over me?" Brittany had the audacity to sound shocked. She pressed her hand against her chest. "I came all this way to protect you, Nate. I'm the one who has been here for you, and yet she comes wagging her tail and lying and you just follow."

Amelia stepped forward. "I suggest since you have more free time these days, you spend them with your grandfather."

"You leave the good pastor out of this conversation."

Smugly Amelia grinned. She might not have the cameras to capture the shocked look on Brittany's face, but it would always be etched in her brain. "Sure I will, if you keep the good pastor out of my grandmother."

"Excuse me?"

"Why else do you think I left the house?" Amelia asked. "I walked in on the two of them rolling around like a couple of rabbits on the living room floor."

With nothing left to say, Brittany ran through the couple's embrace and headed back inside. "Was it something I said, Brittany?" Amelia called out with a cackle. She turned back to face Nate, expecting to see his smile. She got anything but, including a cold chill. "Nate?"

"So you were never fired?"

Uh-oh. She gulped down a swallow of panic. "No."

"I've been busting my ass trying to get you to fall in love with Southwood and you had no plans on staying."

Amelia reached for his hand but he stepped to the side. "Nate."

"And the only reason you're here with me this weekend is because you couldn't stand being at home?"

"Nate," Amelia began. She'd just made her decision to stay in Southwood and now her plans threatened to crumble. "Nate, I wanted to tell you the truth."

"You just couldn't find the time? You've been taking this time off to work on your pitches for more shows. You got my niece involved in them."

"Nate," Amelia said again, trying to reach for him. "I was going to tell you."

"Save it, Amelia," said Nate. "I need to get out of here."

"Fine, let's go. Let's go sit at the bench on the pier and talk."

Nate shook his head. "Nah, I'm good. I need to be alone."

His icy glare tore through her. Tears threatened her eyes. Amelia stood on the balcony and watched the love of her life disappear into the crowd. Heartbroken, Amelia kicked out of her shoes and took off for the beach.

* * *

Nate hated the spotlight on him. Because of the awards, Nate had to get up in front of hundreds of people at the Crystal Coquí Ball and present one to a boutique owner in Villa San Juan. His family might have discovered the island, but it was the people who made it up and kept it going. After giving the award, Nate avoided the questions from his family members. Everyone wanted to know what had happened to Amelia.

"If you and I have any sort of friendship left, you'll help me escape."

Nate glanced down beside him as he stood at the bar. Natalia's frantic eyes widened. "What's going on?"

"I am trying to hide from that man over there." Natalia nodded her head in the direction of a man holding court with some other camera crew people. "He works for MET and he's one of the producers for my show."

Anger seethed through Nate's veins. So had Amelia been using him as well, for this trip, to come here and get whatever reality show news she could get? How stupid of him for trusting her and believing in her. "Did Amelia call him in?"

"Amelia?" Natalia repeated with confusion in her voice. "No, she's been keeping quiet about me being here. She's allowed me to have a normal weekend for once. Can you help me out?"

"Wait, what?"

Natalia cast a nervous glance over her shoulder. "I ran into Amelia earlier."

"You don't think she called her friends?" Nate snorted.

"Friends? William has it in for Amelia. They're after the same seat at MET Studios," Natalia said. "Or at least they were." She playfully tugged at the lapels of his jacket. "So congratulations are in order? I hear she has walked away from it all. I guess deep down inside she couldn't escape her Southern roots."

"What?"

A commotion sounded off from the paparazzi on the other side of the room. Natalia nudged Nate's arm. "I'll tell you all about it if you can get me and my friend out of here. You know where all the hidden doors and rooms are in Torres Towers."

Eager to find out what Natalia was talking about, Nate led Natalia and her mystery man out of the ball-room through the old servants' hallway. Along the way she gave him an earful and he realized more than ever he needed to find Amelia, and fast. He'd made a huge mis-take. But when he returned to the room she was gone—a sad dose of reality he was going to have to face.

Chapter 13

Amelia knew karma was biting her in the tail the minute Cay snapped the second button of her overalls. It had been a full week since she'd last seen Nate. She never realized she could miss someone so much.

"Oh, come now," Cay teased, "don't look as if the last nail was hammered into your coffin."

"How ironic." Amelia waved her hand around aisle three, the nuts and bolts section of the local hardware store, where the Hardware Hottie Bachelorette Auction was being held.

"You're officially a resident again, Amelia," Cay lectured her. "It's time you participate."

"I offered Gregory all the funds to purchase you for this auction. What happened to that?"

Cay giggled and blushed. "He didn't want the risk of someone else bidding on me and having me working elsewhere for forty hours. And with us reopening The Scoop, he's missing me being a housewife."

"Lucky you," Amelia said with a droll eye roll. It wasn't her cousin's fault she was in such a foul mood. It was no one's fault but her own. She should have told Nate the truth. Since Brittany beat her to it, Nate had been avoiding Amelia at every turn. Besides not coming back to their hotel room, he wouldn't answer her calls or come to the door. Amelia had left Villa San Juan with her tail between her legs. But instead of hiding and running off, she was determined to stay in Southwood and see things through. She was invested in the small Southern town.

The crew working on *Azúcar* was bummed when Amelia broke the news to them about stepping away. Amelia had finally figured out what happened at Natalia's secret meeting with Stephen. He was helping her find a new place to live when she decided to leave the show. As for now, it was not Amelia's business—workwise—to know what Natalia was up to. Amelia set aside her mental pitches to MET, even the one concerning the piece about following up with the victims in the Villa San Juan shooting. These were people, not stories. Besides, Amelia had problems of her own.

Playfully Cay swatted Amelia's tail. "They're about to call your number, so go on and work the stage. And remember, it's for charity."

Knowing the funds for today's auction went to charity kept Amelia afloat—that, and hearing Brittany only brought in a hundred dollars for her bid. With a deep inhale, Amelia stepped out onto the stage. The emcee announced Amelia's name and who she represented: The Scoop. A few people cheered. Some men whistled. And then as the gavel pounded the podium, a deep voice boomed through the store.

"Ten thousand dollars."

The crowd parted and Nate strolled up the center. Amelia cocked her head to the side. Her heart lurched in her throat.

"Did I hear you correctly?" the emcee asked.

Nate cut his icy-green eyes toward the speaker. "Yes. And you may as well close the bidding now."

Taking heed, the emcee banged the gavel. "Sold."

A round of congratulatory applause sounded off. Amelia, not knowing what to do, stood still. Nate stalked closer to claim his prize.

"I had a walk I was going to do," Amelia said, squaring her shoulders. She licked her lips when he loomed over her.

"You were going to walk away from me?"

Another lurch struck her heart. "I wasn't walking away."

"And last weekend?"

"You said you needed to be alone." Amelia gulped. Her hands began to shake. Everyone watched them. "I went back to the hotel and waited. You never came."

Nate raised a dark brow. The corners of his mouth twisted into a devilish smile. He inched closer. She wished he'd say what he needed to say. She wished even harder that he'd kiss her. "I am surprised you came back to Southwood."

"You did your job, Nate," Amelia confessed. "You got me to fall in love with Southwood."

"And?"

"And you, Nate." Amelia swallowed down her nerves. "I fell in love with you and I'm not going anywhere any time soon."

Nate took a hold of Amelia's shaky hand. "Is that right?"

"That's right." She squared her shoulders and lifted her chin. "So whatever work you have for me, I will spend my time making you fall back in love with me."

"I never said I fell out of love with you, Amelia."

"But you haven't been taking my calls or seeing me at all."

Nate tugged gently on her hands. "I was out of town. And what I had to say to you was going to take more than a conversation on the phone."

"Out of town?" She felt herself mouth the words. Their relationship was up in the air and he went out of town?

"Yes." Nate nodded his head in the direction behind her. "I needed to pick up something in the mountains of California."

"What?"

He nodded his head again and Amelia followed his direction. There, on the stage, stood Amelia's parents. Had they come for the grand opening of The Scoop? Amelia turned her head back and up at Nate. Instead of finding him looming over her, she saw him kneeling before her. As she glanced down at him holding a black velvet box before her, tears prickled the rims of her eyes. "What is going on?"

"Amelia, I know I wanted you to find your own reasons to stay in Southwood, but I want you to stay here because of me. I want you, Amelia, not for the forty hours of the bachelorette auction, but for the rest of our lives. Amelia, will you marry me?"

Through her tear-filled eyes, Amelia glanced down at her new reality. "Yes."

* * * * *

*Will he be the last
Barrington bachelor
left standing?*

NICKI
NIGHT

RIDING
INTO
Love

Manhattan attorney Alana Thomas doesn't believe Mr. Right exists.
The only one who ever came close was Drew Barrington. Now the
motorcycle legend is back in town. But breaking her no-dating rule
for Drew could also break her heart. Can they rewrite the laws of
love?

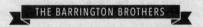

THE BARRINGTON BROTHERS

Available October 2016!

REQUEST YOUR FREE BOOKS!

2 FREE NOVELS
PLUS 2 FREE GIFTS!

KIMANI ™
ROMANCE

Love's ultimate destination!

JUST CAN'T GET ENOUGH?

Join our social communities
and talk to us online.

You will have access to the latest
news on upcoming titles and special
promotions, but most importantly,
you can talk to other fans about your
favorite Harlequin reads.

Harlequin.com/Community

Facebook.com/HarlequinBooks

Twitter.com/HarlequinBooks

Pinterest.com/HarlequinBooks

SPECIAL EXCERPT FROM

H HARLEQUIN®

*Summer Dupree has high hopes for the new
Bare Sophistication lingerie boutique slated for a
grand opening in Miami. Then she spies a familiar face.
Up-and-coming fashion photographer Aiden Chase
brings back cherished—and painful—memories.
And now her childhood confidant isn't letting Summer
slip away again. He's ready to create a future together.
Even when an unexpected threat resurfaces, Aiden
won't give up this time without a fight. Can he turn his
long-simmering passion for Summer into a love story
for the ages?*

*Read on for a sneak peek at
WAITING FOR SUMMER, the next exciting
installment in author Sherelle Green's
BARE SOPHISTICATION series!*

As he approached, she was able to cast her eyes across
his face more closely. Aaliyah had described him as milk
chocolate, but Summer had to slightly disagree. She'd
spent most of her life admiring Aiden's complexion and
it was definitely more like a piece of rich caramel dipped
in hazelnut. His strong jawline, deep eyes and low, neatly
trimmed beard took his look from sexy to downright
delicious. Not that she was thinking about her friend as

delicious. She was just observing a known fact… Or so she kept telling herself.

When he finally stood in front of her, he didn't say anything. She felt his eyes on every part of her face, which caused her cheeks to grow warmer by the second. *Girl, get ahold of yourself.* This was Aiden. Her old classmate Aiden. Her good friend Aiden. He must have sensed her discomfort because he finally broke the silence.

"There are no better days than summer days," he said with a smile, causing Summer to laugh harder than she'd intended. Hearing him say those words brought her back to her first day of kindergarten. She'd laughed then. She laughed now.

"Well, those *are* the best days," she replied as she leaned in to give him a hug. Just like that, the feeling of discomfort dimmed. It didn't go away, but it definitely lowered. She ignored the butterflies she felt in her stomach when they embraced and instead relished the joy of seeing her longtime friend.

*Don't miss WAITING FOR SUMMER
by Sherelle Green, available November 2016
wherever Harlequin® Kimani Romance™
books and ebooks are sold.*